MR. DYNAMITE

MR. DYNAMITE

Meredith Brosnan

Dalkey Archive Press

Acknowledgments

Special thanks to Martin Riker, my editor, for his patience and good humor, and for many invaluable suggestions for improving the text.

Cover: Jun Lee *El Ron* (2003)

"Listen, Daisy . . . ." from *Fernando Pessoa & Co.,* edited and translated by Richard Zenith.
Copyright © 1998 by Richard Zenith.
Used by permission of Grove/Atlantic, Inc.

Library of Congress Cataloging-in-Publication Data

Brosnan, Meredith, 1958-
    Mr. Dynamite / Meredith Brosnan.— 1st Dalkey Archive ed.
      p. cm.
    ISBN 1-56478-353-7 (acid-free paper)
    1. Irish—United States—Fiction. 2. Inheritance and succession—Fiction. 3.
Self-destructive behavior—Fiction. 4. New York (N.Y.)—Fiction. I. Title.

PS3602.R647M7 2004
813'.6 22

                        2003070093

Partially funded by grants from the Lannan Foundation
and the Illinois Arts Council, a state agency.

Dalkey Archive Press books are published by the Center for Book Culture, a nonprofit
organization located at Milner Library, Illinois State University.

www.centerforbookculture.org

To Shana, with Love

'Punk rock? It's a bad scene, man.'

- Frank Sinatra

On an Orient-bound ship
December 1913

Listen, Daisy. When I die, although
You may not feel a thing, you must
Tell all my friends in London how much
My loss makes you suffer. Then go

To York, where you claim you were born
(But I don't believe a thing you claim),
To tell that poor boy who gave me
So many hours of joy (but of course

You don't know about that) that I'm dead.
Even he, whom I thought I sincerely
Loved, won't care . . . Then go and break

The news to that strange girl Cecily,
Who believed that one day I'd be great . . .
To hell with life and everyone in it!

- Álvaro de Campos (Fernando Pessoa)

MR. DYNAMITE

McGrath Reynolds Duggan Coyle Partners Solicitors

47 Merrion Square, Dublin 2
Tel: 1 6684128 Fax: 1 6684167 E-mail:mcgrathpart@indigo.ie

October 11th 1996

Mr Jarleth Prendergast
235 Avenue C
Apartment 6F
New York, NY 10009
USA

Dear Mr Prendergast,

Your aunt, Mrs Lucille McGarry, of 27 Palmerston Terrace, Dublin, passed away on the 3rd of September. We are the Executors and Administrators of her will. You are named in the will as a beneficiary.

Mrs McGarry's bequest to you is £21,000 (about 33,100 US Dollars).

In order to claim your bequest, you need to provide an affidavit confirming your identity, witnessed by a United States attorney and an officer of the Irish Consulate, New York.

I look forward to hearing from you.

Yours faithfully,

Sean M. Reynolds

SMR / nm

FACSIMILE TRANSMITTAL

To: SEAN REYNOLDS
Company: MCGRATH REYNOLDS ETC
City/State: DUBLIN
Facsimile #: 011-353-1-668-4167

Dear Mr. Reynolds,
Your letter arrived yesterday. By a miracle, I beat Martha to the mailbox. She always gets there first. Martha is my wife. She's from Buenos Aires. I tried to reply last night. No use—too excited. I put it in my Secret Hiding Place down the back of the green chair. Got up and reread it c. 50 times during the night. Your good news couldn't have come at a better time!! I was at the end of my rope, no exaggeration. Of course you know nothing about my life in New York. My Years of Struggle. 13 yrs!! This is absolutely fantastic news. 33 grand? I'll take it! (of course to really get back in the game I'd need a couple of mil but $33,100 obviously beats a poke in the eye with a sharp stick!!). I'll get cracking on that affidavit immediately. When everything's settled and we're good to go, please feel free to peel off a couple of hundred for your trouble.

Very Best Regards,

Jarleth Prendergast

P.S. VERY IMPORTANT: All future correspondence about the will to this address:

> P.O. Box 129
> Stuyvesant Station
> New York NY 10009
> USA

NO MORE LETTERS TO THE HOME ADDRESS

P.P.S. Do I need to say how very sad I am to hear about Aunt Lucy?

R.I.P. I was very fond of her, as I know she was of me. I did my best to keep in touch with her the first few years I was over here but then I slacked off. I'm bad that way. I'll get a mass card signed tomorrow without fail. I had no idea she had any money. JP.

Go fax go! - let's get this show on the road - McGrath Reynolds etc? - sounds strangely familiar . . . Sean Reynolds? - I *know* that name . . . Yes yes of course! I remember you Sean: Back in '81 you and Mc-Grath helped me and Mum get that little house Uncle Maurice left us - we had to fight off my 2 aunts the 2 old dingbats from Howth - Thankfully The Force was with us and the Yo Yo Sisters got totally creamed - chalk one up for the Justice League - it's all coming back to me now: that damp dingy semi-detached out in Marino he left us! - Aunts Bobbie and Maxine emerging like krakens from a lake of Gordon's Gin to try to snatch it away - claims and counter claims! - McGrath and Reynolds in their pince nez and wing collars standing firm pushing the 2 old tosspots back - To tell you the truth Sean I couldn't place you at first - I had you confused with your boss Mc-Grath - the tall quiet cute shaver who presented my mother and me with that outrageously inflated bill after the house was sold - but then I remembered: Reynolds = the underling / messenger boy in the suit - back then you were in your late 40s bald medium height horn rim glasses pinky-white complexion bad skin long upper lip sticky out ears tweed jacket dandruff fussy manner not especially intelligent but at the same time quite cunning - up and out to Mass every Sunday morning out of sheer habit married for 25 yrs to a big fat monster wife who fed you rashers and black pudding and refused to fellate you - I must say though re fighting back the Bobbie Maxine Threat you got the job done - and now we're off again!!!! - the gates of chancery swing open and in we jolly go: Ladies and gentlemen wel-

come to 'Where There's A Will' . . . with your host BBBBOB Cratchet!
- Here's the thing Sean: my little windfall is none of Martha's business - I showed her a photo of Aunt Lucy the first year we were married - she barely glanced at it - totally self-absorbed totally self-absorbed - and she's supposed to be a teacher!!! - shaping young minds
for the 21st century (NOT!) - my wife believes she's all about Service
and Self-Sacrifice - Santa Martha del Barrio pray for us sinners! -
Santa Martha my little girl's SAT score was in the 99th percentile
thanks to you so kind and so wise! - I think I mentioned Martha's an
Argy - she turned 37 a couple of weeks ago - the proud recipient of a
Constance Horton Greensleeves Medal for Excellence in Teaching
she teaches Spanish and math to bouncy-bright 7th graders - accord-
ing to her all the kids adore her and she them (one older boy named
Ralphie a bit too much but that's another story) - it's a rare week
when our little apt. isn't filled with fresh floral tributes and crayon
portraits attesting to my wife's superior qualities as an educator
and a human being - e.g. WE ALL LOVE YOU MISS SUAREZ pro-
claims the big handmade birthday card on the kitchen table - there's
a disturbing hint of lockstep conformity here not to say out-and-out
brainwashing but I prefer to take a more charitable view: in reality
my wife is merely a very small cog in the gigantic wheel of New York
Schoolbiz Bureaucracy (her refusal to see this has led to some lively
debates over the years!!) - But I digress: we were discussing the importance of keeping Martha out of the loop vis à vis My Inheritance:
yesterday just after your happy good news letter arrived I was reading it out on the fire escape - I heard her key in the door - Danger
Will Robinson! - I shoved it behind a plant pot - Martha! You startled
me! How was school today? - no reply - just the time-honoured *thud*
of that overstuffed satchel landing on the couch - that night I waited
till she was busy stacking zzzzzs then I got up tiptoed into the living room retrieved your letter from my Secret Hiding Place tiptoed

into the bathroom locked the door sat there marvelling gloating exalting rejoicing - at one point she was banging on the door Jarleth what are you doing in there? - rereading *The Brothers Karamazov* my love - asshole it's 4 in the morning! - OK OK I'll be out in a sec - off she stomps back to bed and slams the door - Prendy counts to 10 springs to attention clicks heels salutes face in mirror exits jakes replaces Sacred Object in hiding place tiptoes back to bed - needless to say I'm acting cool as a cucumber but she knows something's up - when it comes to money Martha's got radar like a fruit bat - yes Sean we have to proceed with maximum caution: the Argentine Viper has her little ears cocked so it's softly softly from here on in with our phasers set on STUN

McGrath Reynolds Duggan Coyle Partners Solicitors

47 Merrion Square, Dublin 2
Tel: 1 6684128 Fax: 1 6684167 E-mail: mcgrathpart@indigo.ie

October 19th 1996

Mr Jarleth Prendergast
P.O. Box 129
Stuyvesant Station
New York, NY 10009
USA

Dear Mr Prendergast,

Thank you for your fax, received on the 18th. Let me explain how things stand. At present Mrs McGarry's will is in probate. We foresee no unusual difficulties but the process can be a slow one. If all goes well, we hope to begin disbursement by the end of February.

In the meantime, please send the affidavit confirming your identity. It is very important that we have this as soon as possible.

Yours faithfully,

Sean M. Reynolds

SMR / nm

———•———

FACSIMILE TRANSMITTAL

To: **SEAN REYNOLDS**
Company: **MCGRATH REYNOLDS ETC**
City/State: **DUBLIN**
Facsimile #: **011-353-1-668-4167**

Dear Mr. Reynolds,
'The end of February.' How nice. How jolly hockey sticks. You might as well have said the 48th of Thermidor or the 5th of Never. It's never a smooth ride, is it? There's always some class of legal jiggery-pokery waiting to jump out and bite a person in the arse. Pardon my French. For some reason I'd assumed this was going to be quick and clean and painless but all of a sudden I'm getting a nasty whiff of Jarndyce & Jarndyce. It's a smell I remember! You recall our previous dealings, of course? You handled my Uncle Maurice's will back in '81. We fought side by side against Bobbie and Maxine, my psycho aunts. But then, after the big victory, Mum and me had to wait nearly a year to get the house!! You said the same thing then: 'slow process,' 'have patience,' blah blah, but of course what you're really saying is 'Hey Prendergast, we want a piece of the action.' All right, Mr. Reynolds. IF you can guarantee to get the bulk of the green to me safe and sound ASAP you can take your cut. Within reason. If and only if. Fair? In the meantime what I need from you is an immediate cash fuel injection, maybe 4

or 5 grand. Something to tide me over till my ship comes in. I have to tell you my current financial situation is nothing short of desperate. My savings are nonexistent. A pack of fags over here costs an arm and a leg. Because I'm perpetually BROKE and IN DEBT I've had to let a number of VERY IMPORTANT ARTISTIC PROJECTS grind to a halt.

What do I do, you ask? I make films, Mr. Reynolds. Shocking experimental animated films in which 'deeply disquieting images of sex and violence intertwine in a maddening dance macabre led by Shiva and Gumby and Sylvester the Cat' (to quote a colleague, Ken Privette). Once upon a time I dreamt of making art using human actors. That dream withered and died. Don't get me started on 'Actors' Egos,' we'll be here till doomsday. Nowadays I tell my stories using puppets; 'PUPPETS ONLY' is my motto. In the end the only theatre Artaud acknowledged as worthy of the name was the mystic marionette theatre Baudelaire glimpsed in an opium dream and as usual HE WAS TOTALLY RIGHT. Puppets are the wave of the future. I don't suppose you're up on the latest developments in digital technology but there are amazing things being done now with puppet animation. THE THING IS YOU HAVE TO HAVE PLENTY OF $$$$$ IF YOU WANT IT TO LOOK LIKE ANYTHING. First and foremost I need a new camera (my Arriflex was stolen). A GOOD camera, none of your Russian rubbish. Either a Mitchell or another Arri. (2) My editing table is broken and needs to be either repaired or (better still!!) replaced. Obviously my credit is good (£21,000). Can I count on you? Are you in my corner? Again send nothing to the home address. Use P.O. box I gave you. Or you know what's even better? Send it to me by Western Union c/o Vincent's Kwik Copy, 64 Henrietta Street, New York, New York 10014. Important: mark it PRIVATE & CONFIDENTIAL.

Best Regards and fingers crossed re my cash advance,

Jarleth Prendergast

I'm having deep misgivings about that last fax Sean - asking you to wire money to Kwik Copy was a bad idea - the place is full of pickpockets and snitches - I know: I have to work with them - the truth will come out: for the past 9 months I've had this horrible dead-end job working in a copy shop - I make $7 an hour - 7 an hr. is a wage beneath human contempt plus the place is staffed by criminals and zombies - the boss Vincent is a nutter - I'm this close to quitting - at the same time my home life totally SUCKS - it didn't always suck - for one brief shining moment about 10 yrs ago everything was going my way all the tumblers were clicking - Trendy Prendy was out every night restaurants bars making connections walking the walk - the name Jarleth L. Prendergast was synonymous with Quality Work in the video editing field - I had a nice car - I had nice clothes - it all went up in smoke - and now a decade later here I am trapped in a tenement dive on Avenue C with a rageaholic wife and a cat who's always stuffing his face - I'm shelling out $360 a month Sean - for what!!?? - a roach-infested shoebox - huge fungoid patches on the ceiling - chronic lack of heat - the bathtub leaks - we're overrun by roaches water bugs mice - Otto won't do anything he won't react he just stares at them - I come home from work totally jacked totally defeated in body and spirit all I want to do is sit out on the fire escape for half an hour smoke a joint drink a glass of wine unwind after another shitty day but oh no we can't have that that's far too civilised: I'm barely in the door and Martha starts throwing one of her mad woman of Borneo tantrums jumping up and down screaming blue bloody murder egging Otto on to scratch me threatening to throw all my CDs out the window - then it's Teary Tears Time: you don't love me you don't respect me I'm going back to Buenos Aires yeah yeah yeah bellow your sick aria witch queen of the pampas bawl and shout till your panicles turn blue - then she locks herself in the bedroom and I have to sleep out in the living room on the day bed - that's my home life in a nutshell: a lurid '50s paperback tossed off by a Goodis clone - all I've got is my art - half a dozen short films - by hook or by crook Sean I've got to drag them over the hump and up and up and up through rotting tendrils of stinking subterranean shit and garbage and frustration up and up and up into the blazing noontide

---

FACSIMILE TRANSMITTAL

To: **SEAN REYNOLDS**
Company: **MCGRATH REYNOLDS DUGGAN ETC**
City/State: **DUBLIN**
Facsimile #: **011-353-1-668-4167**

Dear Mr. Reynolds,
Change of plan: Emphatically do NOT send my $$$$ advance via Western Union c/o Vincent's Kwik Copy. Serious privacy concerns here! Use my P.O. Box instead. 2nd reason for faxing: I was coming off my break when it hit me 'You can't expect Mr. Reynolds to get behind a film he knows nothing about!!!' 100% right so let me pitch it to you properly: the fact is I'm struggling at the moment to finish A MAJOR WORK. It's easily my most intense film to date. It's about
THE TROUBLES IN THE NORTH
I hope you can grasp the enormous challenge this poses for an Irish artist who's an exile to boot. Time and again I've tried to craft a creative response to the bloody conflict that's torn our little land in 2, tried and failed tried and failed, then c. 6 months ago I had a dream. I dreamt I was a child again and standing in my grandmother's kitchen in Bandon Co. Cork. In the centre of the big wooden kitchen table was an orange. Nothing else on the table, just the orange. As I gazed at it in the dream, a green mould started forming on the skin. The mould was 'eating' the orange. The mould was doing violence to the orange. But - and this is crucial - at the same time I knew

the orange was doing violence to the mould. GREEN ORANGE ORANGE GREEN. I jumped out of bed and grabbed my sketch pad and started sketching. In under a minute I had a plot outline and all my characters: The action revolves around MR. SEMTEX, a sinister figure made out of pipe cleaners plasticine and paperclips with alarm clock bell ears. Then there's King Billy, an orange (of course!) with arms and legs riding a horse. The horse is based on Pokey the horse with the black mohawk and insane rolling eyes in the Gumby cartoons (as a European you don't know Gumby, a legendary puppet character on TV over here who's been a huge influence on my work). The other main character is a walking-talking-singing female hairbrush with breasts and long false eyelashes wrapped in a strip of green fabric to suggest a shawl = our own Cathleen ni Houlihan. Early on there's a wonderful scene where the green mould morphs into an Irish wolfhound. Cathleen lets him off the leash and with a mighty growl he leaps through the air and takes a huge bite out of King Billy. As for the Innocent Children on both sides of the conflict, some are tangerines some are brussels sprouts (I have a simple message for anyone who doesn't 'get' the colour symbolism: Kiss My Botty). In some scenes Mr. Semtex is dressed in camo fatigues with a balaclava. In other scenes I have him in a Union Jack costume (UVF etc.). At key points I have him flashing between the 2 - Republican-Unionist-Republican-Unionist - back and forth back and forth over this very weird Ligeti cello piece. Near the end he's run out of Toytown by Hughie MacPeace (a wise old scarecrow who's really the prophet Isaiah) but he comes back right at the end and blows everything up. The film ends on a rather despairing note with this huge sick apocalyptic explosion that destroys Toytown (Present Day Ireland in microcosm) and everyone in it. I was working on this scene when the IRA announced their ceasefire. This obviously took some of the edge off but then they started up again thank God so the film's still relevant. But for how long? If I'd had the necessary funding I could have finished the editing and entered it in the Absolut Vodka Short Film Fest, which would have meant Major Exposure on the West Coast as well!! I missed a huge opportunity there but I'm determined to get

ORANGE / GREEN MOULD: MR. SEMTEX AGENT OF DEATH IN TOYTOWN out there ASAP. My film is a powerful searing indictment of Universal Violence. When we get it out a lot of people will be jolted awake. All those jaded pundits swishing around the Rainbow Rooms in their Prada jumpsuits will be forced to acknowledge there's a fresh voice calling up from the Lower Depths, a voice that may one day inspire a whole generation of young filmmakers. Mr. Reynolds, we can do this. We can make it happen!!! Hoping to hear from you soon with some positive and encouraging NEW$$$$$.

Best Regards,

JP

———————

Well Sean I bet YOU'VE never had to send a begging fax - do you have any idea how degrading it is to have to write to strangers asking for money?? - it's really soul destroying - make no mistake: I'm an old hand at this game - I've kowtowed to all the big boys all the heavy hitters: Mickey Mouse Eisner - Tim Burton - The Quay Brothers - Jan the Svank - Jiri Trnka - whatsisname the guy who did *Akira* - Dark Horse - Pixar - time and again I've pleaded with them hey big boys throw me some seed money this one's a winner I admire you more than God etc. - ONE stinking reply is all I ever got - a patronizing 'thanks for your interest' from a Burton minion typed on fucking dayglo orange notepaper - the fact is Sean I've been spat on and shat on by every major player in the world of animated film - at the same time I've had to watch scores of mediocre shysters panders battalions of limp-wristed egomaniacal talentless arseholes schmoozing (and in many cases I know for a fact sleeping) their way into shows while my work is routinely ignored and even publicly ridiculed - 13 yrs of tears toil and sweat Sean - 13 yrs devoted to hammering out golden artifacts to dazzle the philistines and the phils flinging merde back in my face - it's Baudelaire in reverse - down my bitterness down! - meanwhile I'm struggling to keep body and soul together in this hellhole - for the past 6 yrs especially I've been forced to do an endless series of STUPID JOBS all deeply demeaning to a person of my education and background - hello Vincent's Kwik Copy may I help you? - I'll be 38 next September - 38 is a bit long in the tooth not to have a Critically Acclaimed Major Work out there - in the arts you have to make your mark before it's too late - you have to turn heads and set tongues wagging before old age sets in and the pretty young nurses burst into your room with a tra la la and drag you kicking and screaming into the sunlit courtyard to be publicly fitted with your new plastic anus - after that it's all down hill - next thing you know it's time for your rendezvous with the bird-headed man Mr. Dowdy Feathers who grips you in his iron beak and carries you off to the Palace of Iriswhatsit The Queen of Darkness - down down down into the dust and dark forever - ahoy there Gilgamesh what's for supper? - big bowls of clay - we sit in the dark weeping and wailing and pecking at our breasts - the trouble with you Dublin solicitors Sean if you don't mind my saying so is you just don't appreciate the extreme urgency of the situation - it's the laid-back lifestyle over there: 'Oh look Sean it's one o'clock let's stroll over to the pub and score a big plate of mutton sandwiches and a bottle of sherry each' - no no no: New York's a harsh mistress but she HAS taught me one supremely important lesson: you've got to hit that beach running roll run roll run empty your clip reload empty your clip reload - our eyes are on the prize - our mission is to marmalise the enemy and obtain TOTAL VICTORY!! - nothing less will do!

McGrath Reynolds Duggan Coyle Partners Solicitors

47 Merrion Square, Dublin 2
Tel: 1 6684128 Fax: 1 6684167 E-mail: mcgrathpart@indigo.ie

November 10th 1996

Mr Jarleth Prendergast
P.O. Box 129
Stuyvesant Station
New York, NY 10009
USA

Dear Mr Prendergast,

We are in receipt of your affidavit. Please accept my apologies for not replying sooner.

The normal business of our office has been disrupted by the sudden death of my partner, Mr Sean Reynolds. He was knocked down by a car and killed, on November 6th.

I have reviewed your correspondence to date with Mr Reynolds. If it is agreeable to you, I would like to take charge of the matter personally, to assure a speedy and satisfactory outcome for all concerned. Let me know if this is agreeable.

Sincerely yours,

Aidan McGrath

AM/vo'h

FACSIMILE TRANSMITTAL

To: **AIDAN MCGRATH**
Company: **MCGRATH ETC.**
City/State: **DUBLIN**
Facsimile #: **011-353-1-668-4167**

Dear Mr. McGrath,
Thank you for your letter. That is very shocking news about Mr. Reynolds. We had started to establish a real rapport and then this happens. I'm completely stunned. Yes, by all means, pick it up where he left off.

Sincerely,

Jarleth Prendergast

P.S. I am rather concerned that in the wake of this tragic event my request for a cash advance may have been overlooked. Can you please reassure me on this point?

————

McGrath wrote and told me what happened - I'm still in shock - That was incredibly fucking bad luck - please accept my condolences - I don't know what to say - I'm devastated - I'm sitting here with a glass of vodka trying to wrap my brain around what's happened - It seemed like we were starting to build a really solid understanding then some drunken bastard comes zooming round the corner and WHAMM! goodbye Sean it's been good to know you - I can't believe you're dead - When I read McGrath's letter I had a vision of you lying in a bank of yellow leaves by the side of the road in an Irish Olympic team track suit with blood trickling out of your nose - Was that the way it was? - Anyway I'm very sorry - I hope you're in The Good Place - I'm sure McGrath was a real bastard to work for so all in all you're probably better off - scratch that you're DEFINITELY better off - Vale of Tears goodbye and good riddance! says Sean - and speaking of the grim vale here's one inmate who's currently enjoying a relatively tear-free interlude - it won't last long so I'm making the most of it - it's 1 in the morning - I'm all alone in the apartment (apart from Otto the cat) - Martha's down in D.C. (Washington the capital) - She went down this morning with a busload of her radical teacher pals - they're having a rally to protest Newt Gingrich & Co. cutting Head Start which of course means nothing to you - there was a 2 sec. flash of her on the news tonight screaming at the camera in Spanglish and waving a huge placard - she was wearing that ridiculous patchwork leather coat the one plastered with ancient leftist badges U.S. OUT OF EL SALVADOR etc. - I pity Evil Newt if Martha & Co. get their hands on him (Orpheus ripped to shreds by the Tracian women) - anyway it's great she's gone and I have the place to myself - I had a very productive day: I worked on the soundtrack for MR. SEMTEX and another of my works-in-progress GUMBY'S BIG SCORE sampling from Messiaen / Xenakis / Ligeti / George Crumb / Mott the Hoople plus I completely reworked the storyboard for GUMBY Scenes 5 through 20 - Around 4 o'clock I downed tools and got busy with the blender - strawberry daiquiris anyone? - actually skip that: I ran out of strawberries hours ago - straight vodka shots is where it's at - poor old Sean it really is a shame about your untimely etc. but on the other hand there's a lot to be thankful for - A toast: To Aunt Lucy! - gone but not forgotten - a friend to the poor - a distinguished patron of the arts - God bless her! - at one time she was married to the accordion player in The Tommy Traynor Big Band I bet you didn't know that - and here's to Uncle Maurice! - why not? - Uncle Maurice! - now there's a name to conjure with - the world knew him as 'Mad' Maurice Boylan of Boylan's Hardboiled Sweets fame - he was a captain of industry and a giant among confectioners - at one time he had

300 workers toiling away covered from head to toe in sugar dust in a huge lozenge-shaped factory complex out on the Swords Road - to the family he was always Mad Mossy or The Fecking Fecker - great God almighty there's some serious celebrating going on in the Prendergast crib this evening - shots of Stoli bam bam bam down the red lane and before you can say get down ON it here we are in the wee hours of the morning - I have to tell you Sean I feel an enormous sense of RELIEF: just knowing that money is coming makes all the difference - so I have to wait a few months to collect - so what? - I'll get it in the end - come on Sean you're not at the office now loosen your tie kick off your shoes - it's time that we had a REAL talk - mano a mano shooting from the hip - I have a question for you - cast your mind back 14 yrs: DO YOU REMEMBER ME???? Do you remember me striding into your office all those years ago in my long black leather coat with my ducktail quif / my big bushy sideburns / the 18 lace docs / the bow tie / the morning after tremor in the hands / my youthful rebel bluster??? - I certainly remember you - I remember sitting in your office with a vicious hangover wishing with all my heart that you'd stop yapping - you were waving papers in my face and I could NOT follow your drift - I suggested adjourning to the Bailey or Davy's for a pint but you demurred with that prissy little laugh of yours 'Oh now! . . .' - Quite right of course: go for a quick one with a punk rock client and next thing you know you'll be up on a charge - DUBLIN SOLICITOR ARRESTED CHARGED WITH INJECTING SEA SCOUT TROOP WITH HEROIN AND ROGERING THEIR ARSES - I trust you're not offended by bad language - the breezy banter of the guardroom etc. - in your present condition one would think you'd be beyond all that but if by any chance you ARE offended and you don't want to do this that's OK too - I'm sure there's lots of other Ex-Persons who'd be only too happy to have an interesting friend here on the Physical Plane - so any time you feel like breaking the

connection Sean all you have to do is knock three times on the chest of drawers or else levitate the bed - ha ha - that'd give Martha something to tell the children! - In the meantime here we are: 2 Dubliners sitting together enjoying a drink of vodka in the wee hours of a Manhattan morning - in one sense we're here but at the same time it feels like you and I are zooming down the lost highway in an old Ford Anglia - memories are flooding back - Ah Dublin! Ah The Old Days! - you could still get out of your skull for a fiver - drugs were cheap and plentiful - stuff your pockets with free rubbers at the Well Women's Centre! - punk rock was king! - it was all ahead of us - ahead of ME anyway - actually what was ahead of me was Martha - I didn't know it at the time but she was out there crouching on the far side of tomorrow ready to pounce from cover and take me down - moonrise on the Serengeti etc. - Was she always a high school teacher you ask? - no she was not - my wife-to-be came over here in '79 or '80 and 6 months later married a guy called Bruce who worked for the MTA - or rather he was on permanent disability after a wall fell on him in a tunnel under the East River which caused the poor invalid to drink beer and watch sports on the box all day long - marrying Bruce the tippler is how she got her green card (how I got mine is a much more bizarre story) - my wife stands 6 foot 1 in stocking feet - she is or was one of those supertall Latin beauties - big black eyes - olive skin with a faint green tinge - sangre azul? - downy upper lip à la Kahlo - a long sad horsey face framed by jet black hair now going grey - in the blink of an eye this countenance can change to the lava-spitting face of an angry demon - 'her fiery Latin temperament' - hah! - how laughably short that cliché falls in evoking the insane bouts of white-hot rage my spouse is prone to!! - in her youth Martha was the sort of intriguing androgyne Almodovar talent scouts follow down the street waving movie contracts at - señorita please wait - screen test screen test - you are magnificent mommy but first we gotta know: are you man or woman? - she never became a movie star but she did get her teacher's certificate - Bruce the electrician - esposo number one - ran off with a co-worker back in 1986 - Martha and I hooked up about 6 months later - we actually met through the downtown performance scene - Martha was half of a musical duo with this guy from out on the island who called himself Denny LaBeau - they used to perform at a popular open mike on Stanton Street where I screened some of my early shorts - my wife-to-be would sit on a stool playing really bad flamenco guitar in a matador jacket and cap while Denny - a small pale pigeon-toed guy wearing a black wig with big circles of rouge drawn around his nipples - did an unbelievably wretched screeching impersonation of the great gypsy shouters while slowly stripping down to a pair of red satin boxers - sometimes a second guy - Denny's boy-toy Josh - would pelt the pair of them with walnuts and fresh vegetables - what can I tell you? - it was the '80s - art was IN - I know it sounds ridiculous but some of their performances were really quite moving - especially if you had a good 1 A.M. beer and vodka buzz on - Denny was usually in floods by the time they finished and Martha - my Martha - she always hit that final jagged chord wearing the bravest smile imaginable - like some old-time opera heroine with TB at curtain call - one night when they were packing up I stepped forward and lit her smelly French fag for her - that's how we got started - I'll tell you this: it all seems a very long time ago now - almost like another age or lifetime - pull yourself together Prendergast don't go all knock-kneed and weepy on me - there's a big pot of lovely money about to drop into your lap don't forget - singing happy days are here again - pass out the hats and hooters - let loose the roaring oceans of bubbly! - actually that's a great idea: we need champagne! - I'll nip round to the Indian deli on A and pick up a bottle or 2 - they're on sale

Sean can I tell you something sad? Something Sad and Strange and Shocking? (sit back down on your cloud like a good man)

I CAN NEVER RETURN TO IRELAND - I CAN NEVER GO HOME

But my God you cry why not? WHY can you never come home? - Ans: shortly before I quit the Enchanted Isle for a life of adventure in the US of A I was involved in a whirlwind romance with a witch - a temperamental child of nature from the banks of the Boyne she had long purple dreadlocks and a snake tattooed on her hip - the Young Witch of Trim lived in a mobile home in the Wicklow hills and drove round in a beat up Landrover selling pot and magic mushrooms to bad school children and local farm labourers - all materialistic scoffing aside the woman *did* have extraordinary powers - one day I told her I was off across the wide Atlantical sea to Ameri-key-eye-ay to get Hollywood in a headlock - oh no she said oh no she said don't leave me - But I must my dear - No you must stay here and fuck me morning noon and night - Aw jasus Young Witch of Trim I said would you ever sod off and stop being a leech - Well she didn't like that at all and as true as I'm lying here on the day bed in my boxers with Otto walking on my privates SHE PUT A CURSE ON ME - she actually called me up from Meath in the middle of the night and laid a curse on me over the phone - the Curse has 2 parts but I didn't know about the 2nd part until years and years later - Part 1 is pretty straightforward: if I ever set foot on the Auld Sod again I'll be transformed into a first cousin of the Picture of Dorian Arsebandit in other words I'll be changed into a superannuated moaning undead THING all drool puss cankers and brittle bones mouthlessly screaming trapped in my rotting fleshy envelope till judgement break excellent and fair - the 2nd part of The Curse - no forget that - there is no 2nd Part

- upbeat and cheerful let's keep it upbeat and cheerful

My Jabba the Hutt wristwatch says it's 2:30 in the morning - you notice Sean I don't say 'half 2' - living in America for 13 yrs has destroyed the purity of my speech patterns gimme a TOOna sandwich and a coke said the DOOke of EdinBURG man them cats is blowin' some crazy shit tonight what's this TOON called? - A Night In Too-neez-ya your royal highness - I don't know what happened Sean at first the band was hot and swinging but then WHAM we hit a rogue node of probability and now we're diving down down deeper and down into the bowels of Lucifer's smegma stained underpants giant turd boulders crashing all around us and in our ears the pitiful wailing of hunchbacked charladies huddled around the noxious brimstone pit shivering in their threadbare housecoats - Douse them in lighter fluid! - Yes sire - the wing'd monkeys in their little bellboy caps spring into action - squirt squirt squirt - then Keyser Soze the Devil Himself tosses a match into their midst and WHOOOOM up they go - well those are the breaks and here's the clutch - Clutch clutch clutch me dear unzip your shorts and flex your rear - you must make allowances Sean: I'm operating at levels of prophecy not seen since biblical times - bring me my bow of burning gold / don't be a jerk just do as you're told - I want you to know I would never do anything to jeopardise our friendship - I have deep respect for you as a person as a man as a solicitor as a citizen of Ireland and a ghost of the New Europe but above all as a tireless hunter of fresh young quim - in the prime of his manhood Sean Reynold's Ford Anglia was often seen parked outside Loretto Foxrock with Sean behind the wheel sitting in a puddle of sweat trying to pick up the sexy 4th Years coming out the gate in their criminally short skirts rolling down his window flashing wads of tenners at them Please for God sake get in the car God you're so young your teeth are so white take off your blouse let me sniff you my wife refuses to fellate me - hang on - hang on - I don't feel well Sean - I don't feel well at all - champagne on top of vodka - not a good idea - I think I'm going to heave . . . oh fuck . . . all over her Bruno Bettelheim . . . Jesus . . . writhing bodies . . . mile-high walls of flame . . .

———•———

Do you want to know about Hell? - I'll tell you about Hell - the agonies and humiliations of a life lived in Hell - I know I seem like I've got my act together but it's all a facade - the truth is I'm not a happy camper Sean - Martha the Argentine Viper actively despises me - but there's more - out with it Prendergast out with it - all right all right all right - I told you the Curse had 2 parts - in the beginning she seemed like a blessing but she was actually the 2nd Part of the Curse - Who are you referring to? Your wife? The Viper? - no no Someone Else - who? - no I can't I can't - I can't bring myself to speak her name - you must you must - who? WHO? - shut up Sean shut up - I *will* tell you - just give me a minute to get a grip - All right if we're going to do this let's do it - pour yourself a Winter's Tale and fasten your seat belt

STATEMENT:

Be It Known at the core and crux of my personal tragedy stands a Tiny Female Figure - her name was Amelia - she was only 4 foot 8 - Amelia Garrity A.K.A. The Little Freak Who Ruined My Life - SHE was Part 2 of the Curse - she destroyed my marriage Sean - I left Martha to follow her across throbbing galaxies of pain - she was a thief and a sex worker and a heroin addict - she stole my Arriflex to buy heroin - she had no sense of fairness no sense of shame - she didn't love me - no not one bit as I came to realise - and then to add insult to injury she went and topped herself in a flop house up on 48th St. - she took a dressing gown chord made a running knot in it slipped it round her neck and stepped off the side of a bath tub

- when I found out she was dead I went a bit bonkers - this was my Crystal Meth & Tequila Period - I was drinking like a fish putting all sorts of evil shit up my nose - I bought a gun and went looking for the bastard who drove her to it but that's another story - I must stay focused - Hang on - are you interested in any of this? - suddenly I get the feeling you're not - I see you Sean I see you: sitting there all warm and cozy in that perfect-down-to-the-last-detail simulacrum of your old 3 bedroom house on Sidney Parade - you've just had a nice hot dinner you're in your comfy slippers and your old burgundy dressing gown - the wife's just handed you a nice big glass of sherry - you're sitting by the fire half-dozing watching the telly or maybe you're listening to Louis Armstrong

and I think to myself
what a wonderful world

Oh yes this is the life thinks Sean - but guess what? Louis Armstrong is a liar - a dirty rotten stinking lying peddler of propaganda for The Dark Lords Who Rule This World - 'Friends shaking hands saying how do you do / they're really saying I love you'??? - Give me a fucking break! - of course The Dark Lords Who Rule The Earth want you to believe that crap - they WANT you to sit there hypnotised / pacified / a bit tipsy / humming along with Satchmo - they want you to think this is The Land of Opportunity and The Home of the Brave but of course it's nothing of the sort - when you strip away all the glitz and the babble and the hype what's left? A HUGE STINKING UGLY MESS - this is an evil place Sean - it's staffed by serial killers and rapists and Nazi skinheads and child molesters - all the grunt work's done by catatonic herds of overweight sheep people - the only woman I ever loved hanged herself in a flop house - Martha hates me - Do me a favour Sean: materialise in front of McGrath one night when he's going to bed - like in *A Christmas Carol* - give him the whole chain rattling bit - in other words scare the living crap out of him - make him send me my inheritance or at least get him to send me a decent cash advance - you can do it - get me my money Sean get me my bread so I can finish my film and die with dignity

———•———

Everything's under control - disregard all irrational outbursts - I've just come back from a jog around Tompkins Sq. Park - just what I needed: some New York night air to clear my head - I'm much calmer now much happier - the life-threatening palpitations have all but ceased . . . calming down . . . getting calm . . . yes . . . stay focused on the money . . . I'm going to get my money . . . Hello Otto - Otto the cat is lying on the day bed Sean scrutinising me with his customary insolent stare - the furry football watches intently as I fill my glass with the bubbly antidote - yes Otto you may well stare - I'm both proud and ashamed to report that once again The Old Adamic urge is humming in my loins - Prendergast the autoerotic sex maniac is about to dip into his super secret XXX rated stash of visual aids to emerge with - Aha! The very thing! Starring Marisol and Cheeta and Inez and Dicky Havana! - He pops *Latin Sluts in Bondage* into the VCR - whuuuuur - click! Otra vez muchachas!! - Otto be a pal and toss me my tube of Personal Lubricant

'Our Little Secret'
I pray you Otto do not tell
Mama what you have seen
and I will buy you Fishy Treats
and make your shit box gleam

My God Sean if we can't have a giggle

———•———

Getting up today was a major achievement - I feel like I've been hit by a large truck - I was in the kitchen sipping a Guinness and making eggywegs when the phone rang - BIG NEWS: Martha was arrested at the D.C. demo for assaulting a policeman - she was at the demo and she yanked a cop off his horse so they promptly snapped the cuffs on her and frog marched her down to the station - what's going to happen? - will she go to jail or will they just fine her??? - Que sera sera it's all in the lap of the Norns - anyway it means I have the place to myself for another couple of days - 'Goodie goodie for me' as the late Ella Fitzgerald would say - It's Saturday afternoon and I'm on my way now to meet Gwyneth Raptor in Minsk - Raptor is another story - I don't have the energy - I'll fill you in later - Minsk is a restaurant on 2nd Ave. that has OK mushroom barley soup that they serve with big thick hunks of buttered bread - egg bread - I prefer Vucko's on Ave. A myself but Raptor insists on a respectable rendezvous (living in the past as always she thinks it's still full of junkies nodding out) - Hang on - This is ridiculous - Giuliani el Duce el Mayor speaks: 'Your mission Trendy Prendy is to describe for Mr. Reynolds the million and one little coloured bits that make up The Soberly Disciplined Mosaic of Gotham Life. Do you think you can do that?' 'Not a hope Rudy' - I assume you've been to Czar Rudy's Model City? - Ah you think you have but you haven't: 3 nights with the missus in a 4 star hotel off Central Park - a trip to Macy's - a jaunt through Central Park in a pony and trap - whoosh up the World Trade goggle and gasp - tickets for *Cats Lay Miz Rent* - anybody can do that touristy shit - it's a very different thing to actually LIVE here - to wake up every morning with no arms and no legs and have to buy back your wheelchair from King Rat and his minions by performing unspeakable sexual favours - there are a million stories Sean a million stories - why just last Xmas Crawford an actor chappie of my acquaintance jumped from the 45th floor of the Mariott Marquis a huge vulgar hotel complex in midtown - displaying dramatic flair for once he jumped INSIDE - i.e. in the lobby - diving off the 45th floor balcony like a thunderbolt he fell hitting several jutting-out ledges on the way down - Result = high velocity breakup of the Crawford Mk I - severed limbs flying every which way / bags o' blood bursting in midair etc. - Below = a crowded hotel lobby 6 o'clock Friday evening 3 days before Xmas - 600+ tourists in town to do their Xmas shopping and to see them light the big tree at Rockefeller Center - Imagine: you're sitting down at last after a long day spent traipsing about with the kids and grandkids you're enjoying the yuletide vibe sipping your egg nog with nutmeg sprinkles when suddenly Look Out Below! there's actor's guts / sundry body parts raining down on you - Pandemonium - children screaming - grown men fainting - Security running back and forth stuffing bits of Crawford (he was only 30) into plastic bags - Bienvenu mein herren ho ho ho - Velkum to New York - this is the good stuff the stuff they don't put in the guidebooks - and here we are at Minsk

———•———

I grabbed a booth at the back - I'm wearing my favourite baseball cap the black one that says CUM JERKS in blood red letters under the band logo a fiery ejaculating skull-penis - The Jerks were a band I used to manage - oh yes I got into band management here in the late '80s - believe it or not Sean Trendy Prendy used to be a prime mover and a shaker on the downtown music scene - that was me: video editor by day groover by night - at one time I had 3 rocking combos out on the bar band circuit . . . Minsk is very crowded today - there's the usual mix of grunge kids NYU students marginal types and regular New York families guzzling meat-fat and mashed potatoes with thick brown gravy or fried perogies (dumplings) with sour cream - bored overworked waitresses are muttering at each other in slushy Central European dialects: Z'luh z'la z'loe z'lue - Z'luh z'lay?- Dah - as they pass red hands over steaming red cheeks while over everything hangs a friendly-hot buttery-cabbagy smell - at least they haven't renovated it into a soulless mock-marble fast-food joint like Kharkov down the street - Try putting your feet up on the seats there now! - I've lived in this neighbourhood on and off for 13 yrs and let me tell you Sean this used to be a good old sleazy old druggie arty squatter scene - Now it's all Caffeine Superstores / fancy shoe shops / Calvin Klein outlets / posh seafood restaurants w/ $25 entrees etc. - The rot set in after the Tompkins Sq. Park riot back in '88 - they evicted the tent dwellers and brought in fatso park pigs to shoo the punters off the grass in the name of Public Order - that's enough New York history - here comes Raptor - fade down Oasis fade up Joni Mitchell - Approaching swish of peasant skirts - 'For truly thou art of royal elfin blood my lady' (Vomit)

Well Sean Raptor just left - I lured her up to the apt. after our Minsk rendezvous - she'd never seen the Martha-Prendy pad and of course curiosity got the better of propriety - I said I'd tell you about Gwyneth Raptor A.K.A. Esmerelda Prendy's Bane and I'm going to but first let's join up the dots on the timeline: Amelia offed herself in December '93 - I promptly dived into my Kamikaze Mourning Mode - this lasted for c. 6 or 7 months - I'm quite sure I'd have ended up bludgeoned to death in some back alley in Dumbo if estranged wife Martha Suarez-Prendergast / St. Martha of the Ghetto hadn't come looking for su esposo loco - by the time she found me I was a spent fuel rod Sean - too tired to put up a fight I let her pick me up and carry me back to our new apartment on Ave. C - So by August there we were reunited like Peaches 'n' Herb with all my sins forgiven and forgotten (yeah right) Martha and Prendy Starting Over / Making A Go Of It etc. - Martha's family / all her friends pronounced it doomed but contrary to expectations we kept chugging along - the following spring Martha transferred to a school up in the Bronx and promptly fell in lust with a 12th-grade burnout slash basketball 'star' named

Ralphie - disgusting to see her mooning and pining after a kid half her age but at least I have them on video - her infatuation with the lanky point guard soon fizzled out but know this Sean: Proud Prendy never forgets a sexual insult - 3 months later I saw a chance to get even and I seized it - it was last summer slap bang in the middle of the Great Barnes & Noble / Starbucks Explosion A.K.A. An Exciting New Era in Book-Buying: suddenly Caffeine 'n' Pulp One-Stop-Shopping Malls were springing up along the avenues bright gleaming palaces of acid-free print with high windows to let in the squeaky clean sunlight security guards in nice navy blazers 50 million books-on-tape celebrity book signings by bearded poet-carpenters from Idaho and psychics from New Jersey armies of print-addicted morons slumped in armchairs sporting RAGE AGAINST THE MACHINE T-shirts picking their snots reading magazines devoted to the existential problems of windsurfing - Yo dudes and dudettes! Welcome to the Literacy Boutique! Don't forget with every purchase over $500 on your store card you get a copy of John Grisham's *Golden Book of Courtroom Doodles* and while you're standing there skimming Jimmy Baldwin's *The Fire Next Time* (it's like sooooooooo heavy) lemme pour some of this scalding hot double expresso mocha latté down the front of your designer ski pants - No no far from it: I met Gwyneth Raptor in ye olde fashioned boke shoppe - it was either Mercer Books or Shakey & Co. on B'way or Academy on 18th - I think it was Academy - I was there looking for Jean Claude Verhaeden (Verhaeden = legendary Belgian animator who shocked 1930s Europe with his 4 and 5 minute shorts featuring frantically dancing human turds turds marching in political rallies turds in church turds at the seaside etc.) - that morning my pal Ken Privette had phoned to tip me off that he'd seen a book there that had 2 pages of stills from JCV's long lost masterpiece *Père Jules and The Constipated Villagers* (1937) - Well of course I had to have it so

I legged it up there on my lunch hour - Raptor saw me dash in out of puff - she overheard me ask the guy at the front desk if they had the Verhaeden book in stock (of course the bastards had sold it) - her ears pricked up at the Hibernian tonalities in my voice and - momento horribile - her curiosity slash libido was aroused - I was at the front desk trying to catch my breath - up she crept in her velvet trimmed elf boots and struck up a conversation - apropos of nothing she asked me if I liked James Stephens - I don't remember what I said probably something terse and noncommittal like 'He's all right' or 'Haven't read much of him' - then I turned away and started rooting through the $1 books by the door - a minute went by - I looked up - she was still standing there staring at me - she smiled - like Glinda the Good Witch - and stepped forward and touched my arm: 'Excuse me but has anyone ever told you you look incredibly like John Millington SINGE?' - as in oww oow I singed my eyebrow - give her credit Sean it's not a pick up line you hear every day - to cut a long story short I let her cajole me into going around the corner for a cappuccino - Buried under all those layers scarves shawls petticoats etc. I thought I saw hints of a nice figure - I was thinking 'Quickie! Get down tonight' whereas Raptor had us riding off into the sunset on an apple green charger sleigh bells tinkling off across the sea to Tír Na nÓg and The King of The Little People came to their wedding and they lived happily ever after - you see the incompatibility? The yawning chasm of irreconcilable expectations? - I saw it but I went ahead anyway: the trouble with me is I have this weird atavistic weakness for hippy women - it goes back to my teenage pre-punk Dublin years T. Rex Bowie Elton John loon pants clogs velvet capes tanktops glitter on the cheeks Hot Love Jeepster Telegram Sam - flash a Tarot card at me I get an instant erection - so anyway over coffee and muffins Raptor told me she was a writer - Oh really? How interesting - I told her I was an experimental filmmaker - she went into convulsions

- Oh have you seen *Michael Collins*? - No I haven't - *Far and Away*?
- No - Oh but it's wonderful! Tom Cruise is wonderful! We have to
see it together! - quick change the subject: so Gwyneth tell me about
your writing - she told me she wrote children's books - one had got an
Honourable Mention in some competition - Roald Dahl's nephew was
one of the judges - Apparently it recounted (deep breath here)

THE ADVENTURES OF SEAMUS O'SHEM LEPRECHAUN DE-
TECTIVE

- It was supposed to be a whole series but my publisher dropped me.

Aha!!

The author invited me back to her place for a personal book signing
- This is it I thought: rattle off a bit of Yeats down by the sally gardens
oh Jarleth that was beautiful a quick leg over and then bop on down
the road - that's what *should* have happened but no no as you'll see
Sean the Norns had other plans - back in those days Raptor lived in a
one bedroom on Ludlow St. with a parrot and 4 or 5 stray cats - I won't
describe the apartment - It was full of hippy shit - not HIP hippy shit
just hippy shit - the first thing you saw when you walked in was a
huge poster of smug bastard Sting dressed up as Hamlet promoting
literacy among the masses - on the coffee table in the living room she
had a big glossy picture book: *St. Brendan the Navigator A Voyage to
Alpha Centuri* (of course he got there first!) - she had stacks of CDs all
New Age crap - one was called *Keltic Angels* - the case showed a flock
of angels with long green hair and green wings flapping round the
ramparts of Bunratty Castle or somewhere - there were Celtic squirly
squiggle posters and potpourris nailed up in every nook and cranny
and a horrible minty air-freshner pong - the place was overrun by

teddy bears - she had bears in the hall and on the floor and on the kitchen table and up on top of the fridge and on her bed and staring down at you from the shelf in the loo - she sat me down on the couch with about 40 of them - In a trice Enya (who else) was booming out of the speakers - Raptor disappeared into the kitchen and I got a 10 minute nonstop shouted account of her unforgettable trip to Merrie Olde England in 1985 - The Lake District the Beefeaters Heathrow Airport The Cotswolds Bond Street the Tate the V & A the friendly coppers the rosy red cheeks of the little children and on and on and on - a year later it dawned on her that her *true* spiritual affinity was with the Celts not the Brits - at last my hostess reappeared wearing a layer or 2 less and handed me a cup of stinking yellow water and a slice of 'genuine Irish Hallowe'en cake' that she'd paid $75 for by mail order - Sham Imports is right - she plonked down on the couch between me and a huge ursine monster with glassy eyes wearing a tam o' shanter and a kilt ('Move down McGregor! Let our Irish guest get comfortable!') and proceeded to subject me to an hour-long inter-rogation about my romantic birth and upbringing on the Enchanted Isle - at the end of which as a reward I was formally presented with a copy of her book - I thanked her and opened it at random

'Faith and isn't it a grand mornin' altogether to be going out detectiving in the big world,' said Oisin Owl, who was perched high in an old oak tree. He stood on a thick knotty branch, blinking down at Seamus O'Shem. 'And tell me now, Seamus, what class of a mystery would you be attemptin' to solve today?'

'The Case of The Laughing Shillelagh,' replied Seamus. 'And I'm thinking 'tis yourself will be helping me solve it, Oisin Owl,' he added with a big sunshiny smile beaming through his neatly combed ginger beard.

Oisin Owl blinked down at him:

'Look, Seamus, here comes Mrs. Kathleen O'Rabbit and all the little O'Rabbits !'

And sure enough, hopping hippity hop hippity hop across Rowan Tree Meadow, as darling a sight as ever you might wish to

Enough - I shut the book - Raptor was beaming at me - Grand stuff I said but secretly I was thinking I'll give you thick knotty branch you hippy wingnut - after reading her revolting saccharine crap I felt a titanic urge to fuck all the nonsense about the Little People out of her - easier said than done: the shameful truth Sean is that we've been 'dating' for over a year and she still won't go all the way!!!! - if Martha finds out I'm seeing someone her wrath will know no bounds - she'll rip my still-beating heart out of my chest with her bare claws - and for what?? - 15 months of getting my hand slapped 15 months of coy squeals and evasive wriggling and 'Ooh no! Disgusting! Put it away!' - half an hr ago we had another deeply frustrating sex-tussle on the day bed - I was getting nowhere as usual so I told her Martha wasn't really in D.C. - I lied and said she'd finally run off with her boy Ralphie - it was a desperate ploy to get Raptor to take some of her clothes off but no no nanette Miss Morals wouldn't budge - At 7 on the dot she sprang up and announced she was leaving - she was meeting 'a dear old college friend' uptown - she asked me to walk her to the subway - I curtly refused - smiling and humming she donned her Maid Marion cape and her silly pink wool hat - she blew me a kiss: Au revoir mon cher! - she's on a French kick these days - A bientôt! Till Tuesday cher Jar-leeth! - I barely grunted - I stood by the window listening to her faux-Victorian boot heels clattering down the stairs - Raptor Raptor Raptor. . . . My God how did I ever get involved with such a pompous nitwit?? - I must have been mad - Meanwhile if Martha finds out she'll bite off my DNA dispenser and nail it up in the sacred grove as a warning to man and beast - MEMO: Burn diaries / all incriminating documents TODAY - DO IT NOW!!!!! - Amelia . . . Raptor . . . Martha . . . honest to God Sean I've had it up to here with the whole bloody lot of them - I'm going out to get a drink and play a game of pool with others of my kind i.e. MEN Sombrely Maturely Justifiably Cynical Ennui-Driven Men With Grey Chest Hairs and a Thirst for Beer

———•———

Martha's coming home tomorrow - the union got her out on bail almost immediately but she's opted to stay down there for a week working in some down-and-out soup kitchen - it's a typical St. Martha of the Ghetto move: putting the welfare of strangers before her own husband - anyway I intend to enjoy my last day of freedom - I'll probably drink myself into a coma

———•———

Well Sean how's it going up there on Cloud 9? - I am NOT in a Good Place let me tell you - Martha's Homecoming was disastrous: she found Raptor's headband under the day bed - That was Exhibit A - Ex. B was a little bottle of petuli oil with elves and unicorns on it - You can guess the rest - I'm talking White Hot Fury Sean: crockery smashing off the wall - tables overturned - Martha's a big woman as you know plus she just started taking kickboxing at her gym - so she was coming at me flipping her foot in my face yelling at the top of her lungs YOU DID IT AGAIN! YOU DID IT AGAIN!! LA PUTA QUE TE PARIO!! MOJON! PENDEJO! VETE AL CONO DE TU MADRE!! an endless stream of air-blueing obscenities - Poor old Otto was cowering under the sink frightened out of his wits - I tried to explain that Raptor refused to go all the way but this only served to fan the flames - Upshot of the bust: I was given one hour to vacate the premises - oh the pity of it - in my haste to escape the path of the twister I left several treasured possessions behind including Père Gumby the prince of action figures!!! (I can't bear to think what sick acts of vengeance the star of GUMBY'S BIG SCORE will be subjected to in lieu of yours truly - we have to go back and rescue him Sean!) - I'm in a state of shock - she fucking kicked me out - just like that!! - of course it's all for the best - this was meant to happen - you're not going to see me crawling back begging for forgiveness - hey teacher shove your detention - this is the New Me Sean - you're looking at the New Jarleth Prendergast here - fully independent - no connection with the business next door - got my mojo working - I'm ready to get up and do MY thang - Prendy's on the move - AND he's fully funded (or very soon will be!!!!)

A Message to Martha
You ain't never gonna get it
you never gonna get my CASH
Never gonna get it never gonna get it
Never gonna get it never gonna get IT
never never never gonna gonna gonna gonna etc.

For the past 3 days I've been staying at Ken Privette's place on East 5th St. - it's 2 in the morning and I'm sitting at Ken's kitchen table - I can't sleep - I have a horrible toothache plus the couch here is that crucial half inch too short - I'm surrounded by my life in boxes: books / clothes / CD player / CDs / editing table (broken) / all my videos and reels - of course I can't find anything - Ken's girlfriend Maude is in the hospital for tests (her spleen??) - they're letting her out the day after tomorrow so I have to be gone by then - Maude doesn't like me - she considers me a bad influence on 'Kenneth' (ho ho ho - she doesn't know the half of it) - Why does it always seem to be my destiny to be a world-weary soul walking the streets of New York in the rain?? - Where the fuck am I going to live Sean? - Sorry to be so negative but

I have a huge herpes blister on my tongue & a raging toothache plus I'M HOMELESS - Move in w/ Raptor? Don't make me laugh - Hang on a minute - I'm not using the loaf - what about MY STUDIO?! - I have a little studio in Brooklyn I use for post-production - I'll go out there tomorrow and check it out - where there's a will etc.

———•———

Ahoy Sean Reynolds!

It's 6 o'clock on Wednesday evening - I'm sitting in Firewaters a bar in Williamsburg Brooklyn a cozy public house with sensibly subdued lighting about 2 blocks from my studio (which I'm having trouble getting in for some reason) - There's an excellent jukebox here: I just finished programming a kick-ass selection of Punk Classics - tunes that pick you up by the scruff of your arse and catapult you back to the eternal summer of your nonconforming youth: Damned Clash Ramones Dead Boys Eater Sham 69 WE'RE GOIN DOWN THE PUB - Siouxie & The Banshees Hong Kong Garden!! - THE RUTS!! - 'Babylon is burnin' / Babylon is burnin' / with anxiety . . .' - At the moment I'm listening to Gen X 'into the valley of the doh-hoh-holls . . .' with a pint of Brooklyn Pennant and a brimming shot glass of Jamesons winking up at me - Here's to you Billy Idol ya fuckin' poser - It's good to be indoors - I was standing out there in the rain for half an hr fiddling with the padlocks - some joker slapped 2 huge padlocks on the door to my studio - what's up with that?? - When I catch up with Olegarkis the landlord I'm going to give him a no-holds-barred tongue lashing - I had a horrible day at work - Vincent the boss was in an extra foul mood - He hobbled in brimming with malice - all his foulness was laser beamed at me because I was 10 minutes late - I often dream of dragging him behind the big Xerox and kicking him into the Great Perhaps à la Mr. Sloane - Memo to Self: QUIT NEXT

WEEK - Speaking of persons not in my good books: what about
AIDAN MCGRATH!??! - I see he hasn't changed one iota - he's
still a smarmy emotionless prick - I'd be v. surprised if he's given
you a second thought since the funeral except for 'Fuck Reynolds
for leaving me with all these loose ends' etc. - my gut reaction is:
I do NOT want to deal with him because big surprise I don't trust
him - but with you out of the picture what choice do I have?

NO IT CAN'T BE !!!???!!! I don't believe what I'm hearing . . .

Sorry Sean - I'm back - that was incredible - you'll never guess what
just came blasting out of the juke - 'Peter O'Toole's A Wanka' by
The Cum Jerks!!! - yes the great forgotten neo-glitter-punk anthem
- where did it come from????? - I never saw it on the playlist - I was
the Cum Jerks' manager Sean - they were MY boys - for 2 yrs I
fought to make them An Unstoppable Force in Rock - they nearly
destroyed me - when I discovered them back in '90 they were called
Slypped Dysk - just another downtown loser bar band doing Bowie
and Alice Cooper and Cure covers plus a couple of originals - they
had the shittiest equipment imaginable and no clue how to pace
a set on top of which they dressed like Hanoi Rocks - at the same
time they had this arresting cusp-of-grunge (as it turned out) sound
- Average age of band member when we met = 20 - I approached
them one night after a show - I think they were supporting Johnny
Wylde & The Wyldemen at Nightengales - I was extremely wasted
- I told them I thought they had potential - I can still see that circle
of bug-eyed undernourished faces streaked with ineptly applied
makeup and glitter looking up at me in awe and suspicion - Frankie
Carboni the lead singer asked me where I was from - Dublin I replied
- Dublin? Jeez! Geddoudaheer! - No really I am - Never let it be said
that Prendy didn't know when to play the Irish Card - I bought the

boys a round of drinks - The evening wore on - They loaded their gear in the van (the poor old Econoline!) and we headed down the street to the Telephone Bar - there after many more drinks I told them - put it down to drunken caprice - that I might be prepared to give them the benefit of my promotional skills - they clustered around me all drunk and sweaty - I told them I would take them on with one condition: that they changed their name to Josephine the Mouse Singer (I was in my Kafka phase at the time) - they agreed at once - oh but they were slippery! - a few weeks later they double-crossed me and became The Cum Jerks - for some reason I went along with it - Frankie Gary Timur and Charles: 4 basically decent lads from the burbs with brains scrubbed clean by bong and blotter glue and pills - good-natured stoics most of the time though with a tendency to bare the fangs if crossed or mocked - as I say they were not without talent - I could have strangled each one in turn for not displaying more of it more often but they were not without talent: I believe to this day that if we hadn't been shafted by those evil-hearted vampires at Pompadour Records they might have been contendas (for what????) - 'Peter O'Toole's A Wanka' the first and only Cum Jerks single was recorded (b/w 'Suck On Dis') in under 12 hours including overdubs and mixing (I drove them hard!) in Flypaper Studios up on West 29th - I remember it took ages to get a decent snare sound - during one of the breaks Gary and Charles sucked down a huge bottle of tequila - later G. threw up on Timur's guitar and Charles fell over his snare case and twisted his ankle - God knows how Sean but we got through it eventually - we ended up pressing 2000 copies - I still have 1500 sitting in a box at - whoops! - I nearly said 'home' but then I remembered: I Have No Home (time to leave another irate but dignified message on Olegarkis's machine) - as I say Sean The Jerks looked up to me - and give me credit I did my best not to be your stereotypical arsehole manager - nobody starved - they respected me for that - in the end of the day I don't think they ever quite believed their good luck - i.e. a genuine Irish Intellectual Rocker like myself swooping down out of the blue to take them under his batwing - Of course I played it up - I gave them what they wanted = a connection to Greatness - after a show we'd be in Vaszaks or playing pool in the Blue and Gold and I'd have them spellbound - them and their 4 little girlfriends - weaving wondrous tales of my intimate friendships with Sir Bob Geldof and U2 (I really did know a guy who claimed his sister had sex with Clayton the bass player - she said he was terribly vain and made her shove things up his arse) the Pogues the Waterboys Phil Lynott (R.I.P.) Van the Man the Hothouse Flowers Sinead etc. - I told the Jerks we'd all gone to the same high school - that I used to be Gary Moore's guitar roadie and Van's tour manager - I organised Live Aid - I helped Lilywhite produce *Boy* etc. etc. - well my Cum Jerks were proud to bursting to be associated with someone who'd rubbed shoulders with / lifted pints of Guinness with / done heaps of blow with The Gods of Rock - Of course Amelia Garrity wasn't fooled - not for a second - She saw through my charade - as she saw through most things - it's strange to think I met Amelia through the Jerks (future film historians take note: she's the blind go-go dancer in the 'Peter O'Toole' video) - I never understood what she was doing hanging around that scene - I mean I do and I don't: it was a big full tilt drug orgy most of the time and Amelia loved her drugs but at the same time she didn't fit in - Timur and his girlfriend liked her but all the other women hated her - not without cause - Hang on a minute if I'm going to start on Amelia I need another drink - Let me grab my barmaid with the Spiderman tattoo - I must call Olegarkis again - If I can't get into my studio tonight I'm going to give Privette a buzz and suggest a rendezvous at The Holiday for special cocktails

Couldn't get a hold of Olegarkis so I hopped the L into Manhattan and met Ken Privette in the Holiday as arranged - after a couple of white russians Ken suggested a stroll down 2nd Ave. to see what was playing at Anthology A.K.A. Maya Deren's Tomb - it turned out they were doing yet another marathon homage to the godlike genius of Stan Brakhage - scratch my retina daddy-o! - neither of us had the stomach for it so we went bar hopping instead - over on 1st Ave. at the International we fell in with a charming young woman from the southwest named Rose or Rosemary - she turned out to have a truly amazing gift: *Using only her tongue and teeth Rose was able to tie knots in cherry stems!!!* - I know it sounds incredible and at first both Privette and I were highly skeptical suspecting trickery but then she repeated the feat half a doz. times under close scrutiny - she told us she'd perfected the art while pursuing a business degree at the University of Texas at Austin - she told us about a tower on campus that's world famous for suicide leaps - back in '68 an enterprising young med student climbed up there with an M16 and shot about 60 people from the observation deck - yes we were all getting along like a house on fire until Privette spoilt everything by pawing her under the table - Rose the Miraculous took umbrage and disappeared - Your round I said . . . Many hours later we found ourselves back out in Williamsburg driving around in a car service station wagon with Cindy this awful woman Ken has the hots for - we ran into her in this new bar Northanger's on Roebling - I wanted nothing to do with her but thinking with the little head as usual Privette begged her to join us on our crawl - Cindy's a horror - she name-drops incessantly - every time we've met she's insisted on telling me how she fucked the singer from Stone Temple Pilots - anyway one drink led to another and another and suddenly it was 4 in the morning and we were all out of our minds driving around in this car service Buick 6 station wagon - Ken was sitting up front with

the driver a Dominican guy and 2 suitcases of Bud we'd picked up
from a wholesale place on Union - me and Cindy were in the back
with her dog Raymond a ginormous brute with a touch of the Irish
wolfhound except his head's the wrong shape he looks like a sort of
mutant airedale - he was sitting between us panting tongue lolling
staring with mad lustful eyes at the back of the driver's head - I
turned to his mistress: Christ Cindy your dog is huge - to which
she screwed up her face in a revolting cutesy grimace and started
fondling its head - Oh no she said Oh nooo he's not huge. He's tiny.
Aren't you? You're tiny aren't you? Aren't you? - she went on and
on talking to Raymond in babytalk and scratching him under his
craggy chin - I beg to differ Cindy. The brute is huge - He's tiny
and he's not a brute he's my baby - He's huge - Stop saying that!
- the debate was becoming heated: I was annoyed that she couldn't
admit that objectively speaking her dog was one of the biggest ever
born to bitch - out of nowhere she called me an unfeeling bastard
- simultaneously Raymond started to yowl like somebody had his
nuts in a vice - Leave my dog alone! - I didn't touch him! - without
warning Cindy leaned over and drove her gloved fist hard into my
kidney - the next moment God knows why she flung open her door
and jumped out - we'd just slowed to take a corner - Stop! shouted
Ken - the driver hit the brakes - we all turned around - Cindy was
zigzagging down the street running towards the river screaming
her head off - strange to tell the dog made no attempt to follow her
- Privette leapt out shouting her name and ran off into the dark - the
power of love was upon him as Isaac Hayes would say - I looked at
Raymond - I looked at the driver - Back to 5th St. in Manhattan I
said. We'll have a nightcap and play a few hands of poker and open
a can of Alpo for his lordship here - Woof woof said Raymond and
off we drove into the negro night

Well Sean I'm back at Firewaters - It's Friday around 7 in the evening though I imagine the days of the week / hours of the day don't mean much to you in your present condition - well they do to me: Maude Privette's coming home today so I'm offically no longer welcome Chez Ken - I'm still locked out of my studio - Olegarkis hasn't returned any of my calls - I had a nasty hangover all day and work was horrible: Vincent the bossman is gradually morphing into a full-blown psycho - 'Jarleth! JARLETH!! Did I or did I not tell you yesterday to put toner in machine number 2? I did tell you. Are you drunk? Well? Are you on drugs? Well? Welllll?' - it's all right - I shall be released . . . Yesterday Sean we started on a trip down Memory Lane - it was a big mistake - there's obviously nothing to be gained by raking up the past but as Magnus the Grand Inquisitor on *Mastermind* used to say I've begun so I'll finish: Amelia - that whole period of my life - is water under the bridge - that said I feel a FLASH BACK coming on: If this was a movie Sean there'd be a close-up of my face with the screen blurring and rippling to underwater harps and strings as we dissolve back to the early '90s a scene of domestic violence in a rundown apt. on Rivington St. starring Hurricane Martha and a cornered cowering Prendy - a scene identical in many respects to Martha's recent atomic explosion re Raptor except the Otto hiding under the bed was still a kitten - he hadn't yet swelled into the big furry football of today - Flashback Action Highlight: a black army boot connects with Jarleth's testes as the boot's owner screams:

- You son of a BITCH!! Why don't you FUCK the little cunt if you love her so much?

The answer is: I would if I could. I would if I could. I would if I could if she'd let me ('let me let me let me . . .' a heartrending echo fading into the cold blue distance)

The little cunt = Amelia Jane Francesca Garrity (saint & martyr)

All right Sean you inquisitive spectre you twisted my arm - I'll take you back further - back to The Night It All Began back to the fateful hour when The Little Freak shot me in the groin with her poison arrow - it was a night in late September - we were drinking a huge gang of us in some downtown bar - I was in the middle of recounting some totally fabricated escapade starring me and Bono and Philo and Steve Jones from the Pistols + a ton of coke and a bevy of European supermodels hijinks and bijinks blemming round the Wicklow hills at 4 in the morning in our Porsches and Beamers - not a care in the world drunk as a lord I let my gaze stray down that long wooden table into the trap of Amelia's waiting eyes - a breeze blew out of heaven or hell or both and Prendergast found himself borne aloft by hosts of singing cherubim - a Mystic Curtain was lifted and I was allowed to glimpse the world as a glorious place full of endless possibilities - then the curtain came down the cherubs let go and I fell - down down down into Ye Deepe Darke Poole of Desyre - in other words Sean I fell in love with the little psychopath - I know I know: 'little' sounds patronizing and God in Her Infinite Mercy will shrivel my bollocks to useless flaps of seaweed if I don't retract - but the fact remains she was little - only 4 foot 8 - 125 lbs. (9 stone to you) - even wearing 6 inch platforms and a man's overcoat she was minuscule - she had grey eyes Sean terrible amoral grey eyes and a mocking smile - it was a leer really - tiny hands like a child's tiny breasts tiny cunt full of magic doorways into secret universes not that I was ever vouchsafed more than a glimpse

oh yes it's all coming out now

PADDYSPULSINGPURPLEPENISPADDYSPULSINGPUR-
PLEPENIS

I loved her madly

I loved her madly yet she sank

down into the cold ground

Singing (all together now):

> *Toi qui mets dans les yeux et dans le coeur des filles*
> *Le culte de la plaie et l'amour des guenilles*

(Thou who puttest in the eyes and the heart of girls the cult of
wounds and the love of rags o Satan)

I can't hear you

Fuck off so

Miss - another pint please and a shot of your best sorrow

———•———

Firesnorters - 1 in the morning - yes I'm still here - you know Sean
I really like this bar - it doesn't pretend to be more than what it is
which is a long dark room with a low nicotine-stained tin ceiling half
a doz. tables and chairs one pool table in the back and tucked away
in one corner a really good jukebox - I finally got ahold of Olegarkis
the absentee landlord half an hour ago - he said he was busy and he'd
call me back - who knows if he will or not - meanwhile Crooklyn's
favourite punk rock saloon is getting mighty crowded - some citizens

just walked in with foot-tall mohawks - always a cheerful sight - brings me back to 1978 and my glue sniffing days on The Old Kent Rd. - a moment ago Cindy the looney with the dog popped her head in - I hid behind my *Daily News* - when I peeped out she'd gone thank God - no sign of the woof woof - I'm sitting by myself in a dark corner - I'm pretty drunk Sean - I've had 4 pints of India Pale Ale plus a Guinness 3 Irish whiskeys and a pint of the house's special bounce-me-off-the wall supercider - Be prepared: I'm in a grey velour leisure suit Michel LeGrand Windmills of Your Mind Scott Walker Walk On By sort of mood - it's Amelia - I haven't talked to anyone about her for ages - when I used to vent to Privette he always said the same thing: she's crazy - she'll mess you up - break off all contact immediately - thanks Ken you're a bottomless pool of karmic wisdom - cue Scott crooning 'Windmills':

when she stole your movie camera were you suddenly aware
that the autumn leaves were turning to the colour of her hair?

The colour of her hair! - that was a sore point later on - but first I want to tell you about Our First Date: the first time Amelia and Prendy walked out together - it was the 16th of June 1904 no it wasn't - we went to see *Touch of Evil* at the Film Forum - we bought popcorn and Raisinets and snuck in a hip flask of rum - we jeered at the trailers - we laughed out loud at Charlton Heston's outlandish appearance (it's Black Moses!) - I tried to cop a feel during the Janet Leigh and the bikers orgy scene but Amelia grabbed my paw and bit it - she drew blood too - oh we were both in high spirits that night! - I was deliriously happy Sean incredibly happy - I'd dreamt of being alone with her for months and months - I kept stealing reverent glances at the side of her face - her haunting profile - yes I was happy happy happy but at the same time incredibly nervous - Martha was out

of town - she was up in the Catskills at a teachers' conference - my
rational mind kept saying 'You have nothing to fear' but the rest of
me wasn't buying it - I was waiting for my wife to appear - to burst
into the theatre and come stomping down the aisle in her black army
boots and trap the pair of us in the beam of a powerful flashlight
or - my God - a far more plausible scenario - what if someone in the
audience recognised me!? - I hadn't thought of that - so I sat in the
dark seesawing between the agony and the ecstasy - at last bad cop
Hank Quinlan's great bloated bulk toppled backwards into the filthy
water - pull back - music - The End - lights up - so soon? - No no no I
want to stay here in the dark with Amelia and watch *Touch of Evil*
over and over and over again till judgement break excellent and fair
- I knew Martha was waiting for us out in the lobby - or if not Martha-
in-person then a stand-in-for-Martha one of her crunchy granola
teacher pals - born informers every man jack o' them - oh yes they'd
be only too delighted to report back that they spotted Prendergast
out and about with a pint-sized sex bomb dressed in thigh-high red
leather boots and a fake fur jacket - I was fool enough to confide these
fears to Amelia - she laughed nastily and called me a coward and
headed for the exit - at the door she turned around and shouted

- fucking come on Prendergast I'm thirsty!

Torn between desire and trepidation I sidled towards her crabwise
up the aisle - she stood there leering at me and mockingly grinding
her hips like a burlesque dancer - which of course she was - I just had
time to pull my scarf up and pull my hat down as she pulled me out
into the lobby's glare - we repaired to a bar on Houston St. and drank
some whiskey and later back at her place we did the business - or
about 41% of it - I woke up during the night and heard her crying out
in the living room - of course thinking back it's easy to see I should

have gone out to her and comforted her but the fact is I didn't - it's too late baby it's too late now and the rest is autumn leaves - autumn leaves and auburn hair - Time out: a moment ago a grinning mohawk dropped a shot glass of schnapps into my pint of cider - he claims to know me - says that 6 yrs ago I was his AD on a music video!!?? - it's clearly a case of mistaken identity but I've accepted Jimbo or Jumbo's invitation to join him and his mates up at the bar for a round of submarine shots - it looks like I'm in for a night of serious networking Sean so slán leat agus adios amigo for the mo

———•———

Sunday Morning - Well Sean I finally got in - The 2 padlocks turned out to be the result of a silly misunderstanding: because I haven't been using it much lately Olegarkis assumed I'd let the place go - he claims I owe him 8 months back rent!!! - at our meeting yesterday I disputed this hotly but in the end to avoid aggro I promised to pay him the arrears ASAP - of course I didn't let on about my present homeless crisis - 'OK Jar-a-leet. I give you da keys when you give me da money' - Easier said than done Christos my old flower - but I didn't say that - Instead we shook hands and I tiptoed back here at 2 o'clock this morning armed with my bag of tools jimmied off the locks no problem they don't call me Jock Genet for nothing - so I'm presently curled up in my sleeping bag on the hard slightly damp concrete floor wearing fisherman's socks and my old Peruvian shepherd's cap reading John Buchan by a combination of dawn's early light and flashlight - There's an oil heater here that wasn't here before - no idea where it came from but never look a gift horse etc. - Of course Olegarkis and his brothers won't be happy if they find out I'm squatting in their space - By the way I should point out that this isn't one of your chic sun-drenched hardwood floor 150000+ sq. ft. former factory spaces so popular with the gentleman carpenter class - no this is basically a garage that a candy wholesaler used to keep his van in - 2 yrs ago he went bust and Olegarkis rented it to me - from the outside everything looks the same - except now those are MY padlocks - I actually don't think there's going to be a problem staying here - Olegarkis lives in Queens and he's normally never out this way - If I watch my exits and entrances I think I'll be OK for a week or 2 maybe longer - In the meantime all my worldly possessions are still with Ken on E. 5th (Maude's hopping mad about it) - Prendy's future is très uncertain: a month from now I might be living in Jersey City or Yonkers or - a horrible thought - Staten Island!!! - You never know - You never did know - which brings to mind My Favourite Poem of All Time:

> Down life's random path we all
> stumble as strangers . . .
> You never know though . . .
> You never did know . . .
> You never will know . . .
> So what though . . .
>
> One day, one day though
> whoop whoop, boom-boom,
> 1-2-3 yer number's up . . .
>
> . . . straight back to the House of
> Strangers, for your meeting with the
> Big Guy with the Beard . . .
> the original God though . . .
> then you sit back and listen to the
> wind forever . . .
>
> brr brr whoo whoo
> nothing but wind, forever

Nice, isn't it? One night at that open mike on Stanton St. I used to frequent this gorgeous drunk-off-her-ass Middle Eastern woman was handing out flyers with that poem printed on it - the poet is George Rubin - he was an old New York guy who died in '87 - the flyer said his friends and neighbours were collecting money to put up a plaque in his memory outside the house on East 6th Street where he lived - well Sean I walked down 6th the other day and there's no plaque - I've noticed do-gooder schemes like that have a tendency to start strong and then fizzle out - and of course one has to wonder: when the time comes who's going to shake the tin and put up a plaque for Trendy Prendy??

———

Well Sean so far so good - This is my 3rd night here - The Brothers Oleg. are none the wiser - I popped over to Ken's earlier to pick up a few odds and ends - I was just walking out when Maude appeared out of nowhere and pounced on me: when was I going to take the rest of my stuff? This isn't a storage space I feel that you're taking unfair advantage of us etc. - Chill out Elvira (Maude looks like Elvira Mistress of the Dark but without the bust) - Anyway I danced around her and escaped with my CDs my tapes my boom box and my headphones - I was experiencing terrible cravings for my Scott Walker my Léo Ferré Boy George's Greatest Hits Duke & Trane etc.- seeing as I'm going to be here for a while I'm trying to make the studio feel like home: to this end I've hung my photo of the Fleischer Brothers beside the little round window (you DO know the Fleischer Brothers = Betty Boop - Popeye - Koko - *Gulliver's Travels*) - There they are Max and Dave standing outside 1600 Broadway c. 1924 in their shirt sleeves Max grinning Dave not - I must say it's great to have the little heater - of course this being originally a garage there IS a lingering petrol smell not that I'm bothered by it I actually like it - The main thing is I'm having no trouble slipping in and out - I'm on a very quiet side street and there's never anybody around - Had a bit of a close shave the other night or it might have been nothing: c. 3 in the morning I heard somebody poking around outside - I held my breath - after a few minutes they went away - One of the definite pros about living here is that I seem to have given Raptor the slip - She tracked me down to Ken's of course - I hid in the toilet while he talked to her out in the hall - Last week she turned up twice at the copy shop but I saw her coming both times and ducked - I got one of the zombies to tell her I was out sick while I hid behind the big Minolta in the back - Let me state in no uncertain terms that I have come to my senses at last: I intend to erase Raptor from my life once and for all - The woman has been nothing but trouble from day one - in other words she's all yours Seamus - 'Begorrah! At last!' cried Seamus O'Shem the Leprechaun Detective and Part Time Pimp. And in the wink of an eye sure hadn't the cunning little man unzipped his emerald green tights and pulled them down: 'Behold o mortal dame my candy cane of power!' 'Oooooh!' gasped Gwyneth and promptly swooned (To Be Continued)

I'm sure you'll be pleased to hear Sean I took the bull by the horns this morning and called McGrath - I asked him straight out about a cash advance - would he front me a couple of grand? - He told me straight he wouldn't - Fair enough - At least it was a manly exchange and none of that namby-pamby legal fuckology - no offense Sean - I asked if there was any chance of getting my inheritance before February - Who said February? he said - Mr. Reynolds I said - Oh no says he I'm afraid Mr. Reynolds was being unduly optimistic. I should think we're looking at April at the earliest and then he launched into some bullshit explanation - I couldn't listen to him - I hung up - Which showed amazing restraint because what I really wanted to do was extrude myself along 3 thousand miles of transatlantic cable like Mr. Fantastic of the Fantastic 4 to pop out the other end and smash the phone down on his head - I mean he's REALLY trying my patience - I know the loot is coming I know it's just a matter of time but come on Sean I can't go on like this forfuckingever!!

———•———

Atelier Jar-a-leet Night the 4th
From time to time the thought does pop into my head: 'I wonder what Martha's doing right at this moment?' - Of course I know what she's doing: she's lying on the couch under the anglepoise in her black turtleneck and her red sweatpants smoking a Gitane correcting a stack of Spanish compositions - Otto is hovering around trying to hump her leg and she has to keep pushing him away - don't give up old son friction is your birthright - for the first week I know she was on the blower day and night blackening my name across the world's continents - she called her mother in San Isidro and her father in Barcelona and her half-wit brother the sculptor in San Fran and soul sister brown sugar Gabriella in Caracas and I've no doubt they all said the same thing: what a no-good rotten bastard I am and how they always knew I'd fuck her over again how they tried to warn her and she's better off without me - that Suarez family Sean: a bunch of stick-up-the-arse parvenu dago customs inspectors spoilt priests and back-street abortionists - not one of them with any breeding sensitivity table manners or couth except maybe Fernando the queer uncle who sadly had his mickey mangled by Fidel's boys on the Isle of Pines - Nana the Bent Banana he was the only one who liked me

———•———

Firewaters - 2 A.M. - I'm drunk - You're dead - where does that get us? - NOWHERE - all right Sean stop lapping the waters of Lethe and pay attention - it's time for another exciting episode of . . .

MY LIFE AS AMELIA'S DOG

Where was I? - oh yes I remember: me and Amelia became an item - Martha found out about the affair went ballistic and booted me out - I stayed for a couple of weeks with Ken and his then girlfriend Pippa (a very nice woman - a painter - 10000 times nicer than Maude) - after that I lived for a month in an SRO up on 97th and B'way - the less said about that the better: stepping over junkies every night to get in my door - paper thin walls - nosey psycho neighbours - the whole Hubert Selby trip - at the start of March Amelia got kicked out of where she was living - moving in together seemed a logical step - we found a run-down little one bedroom on 9th between A and B - it was relatively cheap by the standards of the day - for a while I think we were actually quite happy - of course we had our fights - all the usual domestic shit plus she was stripping again and I didn't want her to strip but she told me to fuck off and mind my own business - 'If you don't like it move out' etc. - so there was tension and moodiness and a good bit of shouting and door slamming but generally things were OK or OKish - one night Martha rang up and left a nasty phone message calling down the 7 plagues of Egypt on me and my 'little white whore' - fortunately there was no follow-through and after that she more or less left us alone - we ate a lot of takeout: Chinese Vietnamese Thai Mexican - in the evenings we'd load the bong and watch Hollywood classics on the VCR - Charles Laughton as Dr. Moreau in his spiffy white three piece cracking the whip - see the hedgehog-faced mutants cower and cringe! - Lugosi playing the pan pipes! - Basil Rathbone glaring at him! - make him well Frankenstein - bone stuck in throat - wonderful stuff - we'd go to bars to check out bands and get stinking drunk and shout The Cum Jerks Totally Rule Everybody Else Totally Sucks - we'd go for walks in the park at 3 in the morning and feed the squirrels potato chips

- Saturday mornings were spent shopping in Chinatown midtown uptown maxing out the last of the Prendian plastic - yes Sean it was all rather idyllic in a downtown sort of way - and in a downtown sort of way it fell apart - One Fateful Night we were in bed: Amelia started getting frisky - putting her tongue in my ear biting my neck feeling me up etc. - it was great but at the same time almost shocking - it wasn't like her at all: she usually just lay there in her ice-queen trance and let *me* do all the work - anyway just as I was starting to really get into it she pulled away and sat down at the end of the bed and lit a fag - She said you're probably wondering why I don't do that stuff - What stuff I said? - Like why I never go down on you for example - Yes I said I *had* wondered - I can't she said - Why not? - Because I was raped when I was 13. A friend of the family raped me repeatedly over a 2 year period. He made me suck his dick that's why I can't suck yours and I can't do any of the other things you'd like me to do. I'm sorry Prendergast - I wonder Sean if you can imagine how I felt - An immediate insane flaming hatred for this man this total stranger exploded in my chest - I wanted to kill him - I actually decided there and then that I WOULD kill him - It took me 2 weeks to get her to tell me his first name - Peter - What's his last name? - She shook her head - I kept at her tell me his last name - Peter what? - she kept shaking her head no Prendergast it's not your problem which of course only made me all the more determined to escort the bastard down the primrose path and heave him on to the everlasting bonfire - I kept at her: What's his last name? Tell me his last name - I thought I could wear her down I thought if I kept the pressure up she'd eventually cave in - one night I came home and there was a note taped to the fridge door: GOODBYE PRENDERGAST - she'd taken all her stuff Sean and cleared out - evidently I'd pushed too hard - I legged it round to the strip bar where she was working - the Fuzz Box up on 44th - they told me she hadn't shown up for work and because she hadn't phoned in she was probably going to get fired - one of the managers accosted me on my way out - dark blue suit big oily grin - he told me she was staying with a pal of hers up in Harlem this woman called Cheryl another stripper - you can picture it I'm sure: Prendy's visit to the rundown semi-tenement building off Lex. Ave. - Prendy pounding on the door of the apt. - Amelia open up! I know you're in there! - old ladies in curlers peering down at me through the banisters - waiting - listening - then the depressing retreat down the dark hall - and next day my 20 second phone interview with friend Cheryl: Listen man she doesn't want to see you. She doesn't want you in her life. She's doing fine now. Don't call here again OK? - click - Next scene: I show up at the Harlem address with a huge bunch of violets only to be told that 'the ballet dancers' had moved! - no forwarding address - I made the rounds of the strip joints all the places she'd worked and a few she hadn't - my attempts to question les girls / pass around her snapshot led to several violent clashes with fascist pig bouncers - Prendy grabbed by the scruff of the neck Prendy sent flying through the air to kiss the concrete - Boris the Bouncer at Flutterbyes: And the next time you show your face in here sir not only am I going to kick the living shit out of you I'm going to make you eat it. Do I make myself clear? - as a bell Boris - the long and the short of it was that Amelia had vanished

NIGHT 6: Prendergast - she always called me Prendergast - never Prendy - never Jarleth - sometimes man or dude but never honey baby darling or tender buttons - No - no soppy shit for Amelia Jane Francesca Garrity she was a working-class Irish-American Gen X Supervixen and proud of it - thinking back I'm sure the only reason she agreed to go on a date with me was because I was married - dating a married man: it was a new kick for her - she and Martha only met once - they hated each other at first sniff - there was the huge difference in height for one thing - you know what she was Sean? - Amelia was a homewrecker of the old school - spreading misery and discord that was her idea of fun – Epitaph: 'she was very cute & very mean' - When the dream of love comes tumbling down we rant and rave we twist and turn on our bed of pain we look around for someone to blame it's only natural - after she walked out the only thing that kept me going were thoughts of Vengeance - I dreamt of finding Peter the bastard who'd raped her and killing him - sometimes it was a quick military-style execution sometimes I'd draw it out and make him suffer to the max - in imagination I'd hang him from the ceiling with a meat hook through his heel I'd blind him and castrate him and shove red hot pokers up his bum - oh yes the full *Battle of Algiers* workout - but after a while I got tired of hearing the dying screams of the tortured man-pig and became a staunch supporter of the ONE CLEAN SHOT THEORY: One Clean Shot = a bullet through the head basta / finito / slán leat - in real life I started hanging out in gun shops - being around the hardware had an oddly soothing effect on my nerves - I'd go in and poke around I'd eyeball the pistols the MP5s the Remingtons the Brens the beautiful fibreglass crossbows with night sights attached - I'd ask the sales staff technical questions - but I'd always walk out without buying anything - until one day I met an old man in Long Island City who smelt of licorice - he had a museum in the back of his shop - he pulled open a metal door and turned on the strip lights and led me down the aisle: to right and left under glass in red velvet cases were Colts Mausers Brownings Berettas Lugers Webleys - there was even a Steyr sniper rifle - row after row silent and gleaming - he showed me muskets flintlocks wheellocks duelling pistols from Leipzig and many other curios including a nasty looking ceremonial disembowelling knife he claimed had been a birthday gift to Nazi swine/scourge of the Czechs R. Heydrich - the old guy was a real character - he had German toymaker glasses a droopy grey moustache and an indeterminate European accent - he shuffled along ahead of me humming and sniffling and blowing his nose - he looked like Pinocchio's father - he'd take a piece out of a case break it spin the barrel let me feel the weight - in the end I put a down payment on a .38 Smith & Wesson revolver with a cherry red plastic grip - well Sean his face lit up he said it was a good gun I'd be very happy with it - happiness is a warm gun I said but of course he didn't get the reference - I went back 2 days later and handed over the balance - $375 - he wouldn't let me leave without a lecture on proper care and cleaning - he threw in a box of bullets free gratis and a pamphlet on how to cherish your weapon written in Serbo-Croatian (?) plus his business card which I subsequently lost - 'Call me if you have problem. Have a nice day' - I left with Mr. Cherry Red in a nice black leather case lined with green velvet - 'Green because you are broth of boy' - OK so I'd scored my piece - next step: FIND PETER AND KILL HIM - easier said than done - what did I have to go on? Practically zilch: I didn't know where he worked I didn't know where he lived I didn't know what he looked like in fact I knew nothing about him at all - mulling it over one night it suddenly occurred to me that he was probably from Inwood too - Inwood? says Sean - What is Inwood? - Alright you asked for it - here it comes . . . AMELIA'S MISERABLE IRISH AMERICAN CHILDHOOD: Amelia Jane Francesca Garrity was born in 1968 or 1969 or 1970 (she was v. cagey about her exact DOB) - she grew up in Inwood which is - or was - a big Irish enclave in North Manhattan - when she was 4 she told me her sainted mother Eileen died in childbirth leaving her and new little sis Patty to cope with Da a red-faced boorish bitter alcoholic who worked for Con Ed and beat his daughters every night with a table tennis bat or a baseball bat or a canoe paddle I can't remember which - after administering the nightly ritual thrashing Dan Garrity - for that was the tyrant's name - Dan liked to sit at the kitchen table w/ a bottle of Bushmills listening to the Wolfe Tones the Clancy Bros. Nana Mouskouri Tom Jones etc. looking at faded snapshots of

his dear dead spouse: Eileen in a bikini smiling at the beach c. 1973
- Eileen looking lovely at a Knights of St. Killian Dinner Dance 1972
etc. - after a while Dan would begin to weep and bang his great hairy
fists on the table cursing all the saints in heaven for his miserable
lonely lot - then he'd chug down the last of the Bushmills and nod off
and start snoring - Amelia and Patty would have to tiptoe around
the apt. holding their breaths communicating in dumb show - upon
waking Dan would be understandably befuddled and bad-tempered
- he would loudly demand his supper - and woe betide Amelia and
Patty if it wasn't ready and cooked just right because he'd start dol-
ing out more slaps and wallops soon as blinking - Big Dan Garrity
who gave religiously to 'The Cause' and wanted his daughters to be
champion Irish dancers - Big Dan Garrity with his guilty skirt-chas-
ing and his periodic fits of drunken rage when he wrecked the apartment causing the 2 little girls to flee for their lives and hide out with
the nice Jewish lady down the hall till Danny boy passed out again
and the coast was clear - and thus Amelia grew from a wee scared
child into a teenage girl - at which point enter Peter the Rapist - Inwood he must live up in Inwood I decided - so every day for 2 weeks I
took the A train up the island and hung out in the shops and bars of
the nabe trying to get a lead - I interviewed a slew of barmen shop-
keepers barbers drunks + wastrels - my cover story was that I was a
son of Erin named Paddy Prendergast fresh off the boat and looking
for my fourth cousin Peter whose last name I couldn't remember
because I'd lost my address book at JFK ah sure you know yourself
- yes a highly improbable tale and apparently believed by all - What
age is this Peter guy? they'd ask me - about 40 I'd say acting on my
hunch that he was a pal of Dan the da - Peter . . . 40? . . . puzzled
frowns and heads shaking all round - strange to say the name Dan
Garrity rang no bells either - so much for the myth of the tight-knit
immigrant community! - on my last Inwood trip but one I finally did
meet a Peter - 81-year-old Peter Prendergast from Tralee via Bristol

and Philadelphia - he was a wizened old coot in a tweed cap 5 foot 2 with a mad gleam in his eye: 'So you're from Dublin are you? Well I spit on you in that case!' - mad senile laughter - 'Will you have another pint Peter?' - 'I will. Dublin Prendergasts! Pah! Stuck up pricks the lot o' youse! West Brit fuckin' blueshirts that wouldn't give you the steam off their piss—' - The old charmer continued in this vein for fully half an hour raking my forebears over the coals with his Adam's apple doing a little gig and the barman staring out the window picking his nose and Bing crooning 'White Christmas' on the radio - no Sean Inwood was a dead loss - I stopped taking the A train - Things looked hopeless - one afternoon during a thunderstorm I ducked into St. Pat's - I'd never been inside the great cathedral - I lit a candle and asked the Blessed Virgin to help me - just like that: 20 yrs of cheerful atheism down the drain!!! - Holy Mary Mother of God I know in the past I have failed to show you the respect and honour that is your due especially in view of your interesting origins in pre-Christian fertility cults cf. R.Graves and others but please if you can overlook this lapse smile down upon your wayward son give me strength for the task ahead and in return I promise to straighten up and fly right - O BVM in your powder blue gown bring me the head of Peter the Rapist - or rather let me bring YOU the head - Mystery Lady Disco Lady Star of the Sea & Queen of All The Salty Sailors HELP ME amen - Fighting words you might say but deep down Sean I knew I'd gone off the boil: deep down I knew I'd never find him - a few weeks later at the tail end of a serious 3 day batter I met a shady character in a laundromat on Ave. B who told me his name was Alonzo - I have no idea what he was on - I was pretty wasted too - while repeatedly knocking our heads together we negotiated a swap: in exchange for my .38 he promised to supply me with (a) a generous quantity of marching powder (b) a big bag of topnotch grass and (c) an introduction to 2 young ladies in matching tan halter tops who he claimed were his nieces - I still have their photo in my wallet - he swore to me they were both 18 and international supermodels and ready willing and able to party all night long with a virile man of distinction like myself - the deal fell through at the last minute - not surprising considering the condition both of us were in - but the point is I came this close to swapping my rod for drugs and sex - proof positive that my dedication to The One Clean Shot Theory had waned - still I'm glad I didn't sell Mr. Cherry Red - because you never know do you? - After I lost his nice black case I made a holster for him out of pink bubble wrap - all the time at Martha's he lived quietly in my hidey hole down the back of the green chair and Teacher Teacher was none the wiser - and Mr. Cherry Red is here with me tonight in my studio safely tucked away on the shelf above the door with the tins of primer and the rat poison and the rusty jigsaws - he's asleep right now - I wonder who he's dreaming about?

———•———

Night X: Oh Sean Sean Sean it was a mistake to rake up the past - I don't blame you I blame myself but now I can't turn the shit off - it's all McGrath's fault: come on McGrath you fuck-dog get up off your bloated backside and send me my $$$$$$ so I can finish my film - one more time it's called ORANGE/GREEN MOULD: MR. SEMTEX AGENT OF DEATH IN TOYTOWN an animated feature conceived written & directed by Jarleth L. Prendergast for Artaud's Hiding In The Forest With A Bow & Arrow Productions - if I could just get back to work Sean old buddy old stiff I wouldn't be spending all my time brooding on these sordid shameful memories - I wouldn't have to get shit-faced drunk every night - well actually I would because it's the only way I can face going back to sleep in a stinking damp garage full of deadly petrol fumes after my wife a self-righteous Argy cunt threw me out on my ear by Christ I wish I was dead

———•———

McGrath Duggan Coyle Partners Solicitors

47 Merrion Square, Dublin 2
Tel: 1 6684128 Fax: 1 6684167 E-mail: mcgrathpart@indigo.ie

November 25th 1996

Mr Jarleth Prendergast
P.O. Box 129
Stuyvesant Station
New York, NY 10009
USA

Dear Mr Prendergast,

In the matter of your bequest, I am afraid I have some bad news.

Early last week, a later version of Mrs McGarry's will was submitted to probate. The document's validity has now been established beyond doubt. Under the provisions of this new will, the main beneficiaries are your two aunts, Mrs Maxine McLaughlin and Mrs Roberta Clifton. You are mentioned in the will, but not as a main beneficiary.

Your aunt's bequest to you is a handsome bone china teapot. The stamp on the bottom identifies it as a product of the Midlands Clayworks, Arklow. In her will, Mrs McGarry refers to the teapot as being of great sentimental value. Apparently it was a favourite plaything of yours when you were a child.

Obviously, from your point of view, these provisions are a good deal less satisfactory than those of your aunt's previous will. In the circumstances, we will be happy to bear the cost of sending the teapot to you.

Please confirm that your present post office box address is a suitable reception point for a package marked 'Fragile'.

Yours faithfully,

Aidan McGrath

AM/vo

––––•––––

WHERE WERE YOU SEAN??? - I thought you had my back! - evidently not: while you were flying around attending heavenly garden parties your former employer dropped a BOMB on me - I've been REAMED Sean REAMED violated 10 ways to Sunday by McGrath and the Nympho Dipso YoYo Sisters - I should have known something like this was going to happen - I never trusted that bastard for a second as well you know - Fucking Bobbie and fucking Maxine - they must have done a hell of a number on Lucy to turn her against me - and what little bone shall we toss to Jarleth? - some antique silverware that might fetch a few bob? - a nice gold ring? - No Sean she left me a TEAPOT - 'favourite plaything'???? - I have absolutely no recollection of the vile object - the whole thing stinks Sean - it stinks to high heaven - it's totally cooked - I mean it's clearly a put up job - new will???? - there's NO WAY this could have happened without deep collusion between McGrath and the 2 black widows - he's standing there grinning flashing them the 2 thumbs up while the 2 old witches give it to me in the butt - I mean where's the cosmic justice I was promised at my christening? - hush hush my child don't be a silly boy and make a scene! - oh dear was I being silly aunties? in that case please do continue - and McGrath!!?? - he didn't even have the decency to apologise for jerking me around for 3 months - clearly the man's a total wanker - how did you stand working for him? - I hope there was no secret buggery going on - desktop rogering after the cleaning lady went home etc. - Of course I know what I have to do: I've got to hop on a plane and fly back to Dublin immediately and confront them with their evildoing - give THEM a nasty shock - I'll rent a car and drive out to Howth - I'll sneak up on their rose-trimmed cottage when they're both lying passed out at the dinner table after multiplying the cups - I'll yank out their Cork Dry Gin drips tie them up gag them and carry them up to the attic - cut off from their supply we'll see how long they hold out!! - Watch me now: strutting up and down before my 2 dear aunties singing lewd songs passing gas trumpetingly tormenting & tantalizing them with delicious mixed drinks which I lovingly describe as I concoct but only let them sniff!!! - as the DTs sets in on the third or fourth day I can see them caving in completely - yes on Day 3 of the siege all resistance crumbles - final scene: me beaming in triumph as Maxine and Bobbie sign special papers handing everything over to me - and because I'm not a totally heartless conqueror I do keep my promise and reward my prisoners with a small glass of dry sherry each . . . who am I kidding? - they won - I can't touch them - the best I can do is shout at them on the phone long distance - which is completely pointless and pathetic - this is a horrible nightmare Sean: yesterday I had everything today I have nothing - I'm right back where I started - except it's worse now far worse because I was actually within sight of Shangri-La but then the fucking Yeti appeared swinging a huge ice club and chased me down the mountain - a fucking teapot Sean for shame

An hour ago there was a huge explosion about 2 inches from my head - I was asleep in the sleeping bag - BOOOOOOM!!!!! - I jumped up - totally deaf in total darkness - I groped over to the little window - I climbed up on the milk crate and peeped out: there was a gang of kids out on the street setting off cherry bombs and M80s - The cops came and they ran away but dozens of car alarms are still going off and all the dogs in Williamsburg are barking and I know I won't be able to get back to sleep which is just as well because I was having a horrible nightmare: in my dream I was back in the seventh city being chased through the old Dandelion Market by a gang of Egyptian mummies - the mummies were howling and screaming and their bandages were unravelling and disgusting pink pus was oozing out - of course Maxine and Bobbie were leading the pack - there was an anvil or something incredibly heavy tied to my leg so I couldn't run - I crawled under one of the vendor's tables to get away from them but of course they were under there too reaching up with their rotting fingers to snuff me out - suddenly the scene changed - I was standing in the middle of my old school rugby pitch - the rest of the team had gone back to the togouts all cursing me because I should have scored a try and won the match but instead I panicked and kicked to touch and the other side won - something that actually happened to me when I was 8 - in the dream it was getting dark and it was drizzling - I looked back at the goalposts and I saw Fr. Stanley standing beside the left post with Sam the groundsman - Sam was bent over - it was dark and I couldn't make out what he was doing - I went over to them walking around the puddles - when I got closer I saw Sam had a shovel - he was digging up the post - Fr. Stanley was directing him - I said 'Fr. Stanley why are you taking the posts down?' - 'Because we can't reach her with the ladder. She's too high up' - he pointed and of course there was Amelia hanging from the crossbar

———•———

Garage / Night - Raging toothache - no Advil - can't sleep - I'm on the hell train Sean: first Martha throws me out then Maxine and Bobbie my supposed own flesh and blood gyp me out of my inheritance - What next? - where's the next axe blow going to fall?? - maybe tomorrow or the next day Vincent will go stark raving mad: 'All you zombies all you sales clerks and photocopiers now hear this: I command you to seize the slacker Prendergast and bind him fast! He's of no use to anyone so tonight at the stroke of midnight I mean to offer him up as a sacrifice to the Great God Minolta!' - and you know the zombies would fucking do it too - from the pain of the present Sean my mind flees like a wounded fawn - where do I end up? - not standing by some tranquil forest pool gazing at my sad reflection - no: I race down dark tunnels hung with grinning ivy . . . into the past . . . 3 months after she left me I ran into Amelia on West B'way - she came swanning towards me arm wrapped around Dave Drake a shifty-eyed trustafarian twit who 'wrote' a column for *Twirl* the rock rag - they were both way gone - Garrity's eyes had that telltale heroin sheen but other than that she looked amazing: her hair was teased up in a beehive she was wearing the Chinese silk shirt I bought her in Chinatown with the red dragons on it over a black vinyl bra - we stopped to chat - it was incredible Sean: here was the woman who'd walked out on me without so much as a see ya round - who'd blithely disappeared off the face of the earth for 3 months while I got stomped on and pissed on by thug bouncers trying to find her - and suddenly there we were chatting in the street as if nothing had happened!!! - Dave was grinning at me with stoned condescension while I mouthed inanities and nodded like a fool - suddenly I was filled with passionate and bitter longing - I wanted to make love to her right there and then - to hump her cross-eyed on the pavement with her skirt up over her head - to spend howling and then melt into thin air - Horniness is a terrible thing - you can't reason with it - ask the monks of old in their cells ask the succubi and incubi loitering in dark corners waiting for Brother Innocent to drop into REM or Mother Agnes to start snoring over her beads - meanwhile Dave was standing there grinning at me - all right arsehole so you think I'm funny do you? - Cruunch! - Prendy dropped the caitiff hound with a knee to the goolies - Amelia started screaming and swinging at me with her beach umbrella - Dave was on the ground knees to chest but to my surprise he got up and pulled out a toy flick knife - Pathetic gesture! - the Prendian boot slammed whumph! into his tummy tum tum - on your knees varlet - I was about to dole out some more Wu Tang / Beach Hill Boot Boys Rule OK ultra violence when the next thing I knew I was grabbed from behind by 2 foreign goody goody types Danes or Swedes - my arms were pinned to my sides and all at once there was this annoying My-English-Is-Good voice droning in my ear 'Hey man easy hey chill out OK?' - let me go you Aryan mongoloids she belongs to me how dare you interfere - 'Cool it man! Cool it . . . Walk on. We'll hold him here' my attackers told Amelia and smirking Dave - so the happy heroin couple started walking away and all I could do was bellow horrible threats and obscenities after them at the top of my lungs - Amelia spun on her heel at 10 yds. and gave me the finger eyes blazing enmity through the dope I HATE YOU - fair enough sweetheart ditto with knobs on - I watched them turn the corner as the Scandinavians marched me off in the opposite direction chitchatting to me about soccer and how nice it was to get a game in Central Park on a summer's day and what part of Ireland was I from and the World Cup oh yeah man how thrilling it was when Ireland beat Romania - come off it lads as if any of that mattered - actually in the end the 2 Svens turned out to be quite good company: the 3 of us repaired to Fanelli's - travelers checks were produced and we got completely hammered in no time

About 6 weeks after I sorted out Grinning Dave I ran into her again - this time on 6th Ave. - Sean I thought I was dreaming - she'd dyed her hair blue - Her beautiful auburn hair was BLUE - I stared at her: What next I thought an eyebrow staple / a knitting needle rammed through the tongue and out the jaw? - Her face was puffy and pale she had a hacking cough she looked like shit - all from fucking drugs - and she was weirdly friendly - she seemed to have no recollection of our last meeting - I gathered she'd given Dave the shove - she said she was stripping at Snatches and 2 other places - 'I'm making huge shit piles of money Prendergast' - Yeah I felt like saying and I know where it's going too - you're not a dabbler any more my dear no you're clearly A User - As she walked away I stood looking after her - I remember thinking maybe she dyed her bush as well - Was it blue too? - I had a vision of the lips of her vulva dyed blue and studded with little rings that made her jingle in the sack now - she went walking away from me up 6th Ave. in her high-heel clogs - yes Sean I stood and watched the only woman I have ever loved disappear up the street - a freaky little midget in skin-tight vinyl trousers a green angora sweater and silver high-heel clogs - and that was the last time I saw her

Actually the last time I saw her was in the Strand - I was in there one afternoon nosing around - I was flicking through that book of dirty photos *New York Girls* and lo and behold there she was - bound and gagged and tied to a kitchen chair with this skanky bleach blonde in a rubber mini skirt licking her earlobe and tweaking her nipple - I was so upset I walked out and left all my stuff in the bag check

---

Night XXX - wine of Advil

The catholic church did a number on us Sean - We can shake our invisible chains and weep and moan and thrash about on the floor of the stable in Bethlehem weep and moan and thrash about all night on the filthy floor with the animals looking on in embarrassment but never again will we find the strength to rise up singing out of the muck and walk out into the swaying fields of blazing golden daffodils with the warm summer breeze blowing through our blue hair to make marvelous full-blown erotic love in the bonny wild gorse and rolling heather 2 freed souls voluntarily fucking and sucking in a stupendous exploding nimbus of light and free-form pagan God-consciousness

---

I think I mentioned I had a tooth that was killing me - today I went to the dentist - there's a cheap clinic on 3rd between C and D that Martha turned me on to yrs ago - It's not a bad place if you don't mind sitting for hours hemmed in on all sides by drooling old men and distemperish babies - Of course I put off going till the last minute: last night the whole left side of my face swelled up like a football so I had to take action (my condition isn't helped by the fact that I go to sleep every night inhaling poisonous petrol fumes) - Anyway the dentist Dr. Ng poked around for a minute and then told me he was very disappointed with me (they do that over here - the little scolding then the lecture on flossing) - To cut a long story short he had to yank 2 of my side teeth - 2 molars - Apparently the root canals I got back in '88 had broken down beyond repair (thank you rotten smiley-face New Age dentist) - Anyway as it turned out the actual yanking part didn't really hurt at all thanks to the anesthetic they gave me on top of a wee precautionary nip of Remy Martin I had in the elevator going up - What was hard was the waiting - very hard on the nerves – having to sit there and watch Dr. Ng and his fat but attractive Latina assistant rummaging around on that big steel tray selecting the instruments of torture - as the anesthetic started to kick in I became aware that there was a radio on in the next room - I listened rapt - the great Lou Rawls was singing:

love
is a hurtin' thing
love
is a hurtin' thing

The assistant nudged the dentist and told him that the patient was crying - Dr. Ng all solicitous leaned over me blinking down at me from behind his orange plastic welder's goggles and his antiAIDS mask - 'If you wish we can postpone the extraction for another time' - No I said I'm all right really. Yank away doc yank away - Lou Rawls was strumming my pain with his fingers - actually with his larynx - but I wasn't going to tell them that - No no proud Prendy dried his eyes and bid them do their worst

———————

Studio / Night
So sweet so cold so fair - I'm having a terrible attack of The Wine Griefs tonight Sean - I know from long experience there's no use fighting it so I've surrendered - I'm sitting here in my studio-garage getting completely shitfaced by candlelight - I'm making a tape - not just any old tape this is Thee Definitive Compilation of Unbearably Sad Love Songs:

You can't put your arm around a memory
No you can't put your arm around a memory

You can't put your arm around a memory
Don't try
Don't try

Viva Johnny Thunders - who on earth is Johnny Thunders? asks
Sean - it doesn't matter - Not all the songs on my tape are sad or
love songs per say but they're all actually both in as much as they
all remind me of Her - e.g. Side 2 will kick off with an old fave rave
of Amelia's - ANGEL BOOTY by Benito Tafkap & The Butthump-
ers - 'Spread 'em baby! / Heavenly baby! / Uh-HUH! / Uh-HUH
Uh-HUH!' - Amelia liked B. Tafkap because quote 'all his songs
are about fucking or dying' - she was cute as a button with her pop
pronouncements - Side 1 Song 4: Frank Sinazi Live in Lost Wages
singing 'The Shadow of Your Smile' - 'Here's a purdy song - a bran'
noo song as a madder of fact . . .' - cut the crap Sinazi just sing the
bloody thing - all in all it's shaping up to be a full-tilt sludge bath
of Nostalgia-Anguish-Tears-Regrets - at the controls tweaking the
knobs and setting the toxic levels is that tragic figure from Irish
folklore the Comte de Monte Prendergast attended as ever by his
loyal pair of headphones - we've killed 2 bottles of wine me boys
and there's only a couple of inches left in number 3 - I should have
bought more booze - wait a minute I've just remembered WE HAVE
BACKUP there's a half bottle of vodka up on the shelf - I've recently
made friends with the guys in the liquor store on Bedford Ave. - I
expect to have a tab going there v. soon - There - c'est un fait accompli:
I did what I swore I would not do - I just put on Trane & Duke - 'In
A Sentimental Mood' - 'In A Sentimental Mood': are you aware that
Coltrane wasn't satisfied with the take? - Of course you're not but
it's true: he wanted to do it again - he was out of his mind that John
Coltrane - of course once on the slippery jazz ballad slope there's no
stopping there's no going back

'Embracable You'
'Gloomy Sunday'
'All the Things You Are'
'It Had to Be You'
'Every Time We Say Goodbye'
and so on and so on

until I'm in tears which is what I wanted

———•———

Studio - Anytime - we live in hell Sean - These are the songs I sing to keep my spirits up:

BLUES RANT No. 6
I live in a garage
Said I live in a garage
this is not a studio
no no it's a poorly ventilated garage
and where I come from
it's pronounced GARRIDGE
and we don't say 'stoodio' either
no no we're one step ahead of you bastards
we say woo foo fuck
Woo Foo Fuck

Chorus:
So sod off you bastards
and leave me alone
I say sod off and leave me alone

At work the zombies roll their eyes
they say 'He smells like gasoline'

snooty little bastards
snotty little bastards
they don't care
if the fumes are killing Prendy
petrol fumes gonna kill poor Prendy
I'm having an asthma attack
I'm having an asthma attack
I can't breathe
I feel like I'm dying
I'm lying here in the dark
in this rotten stinking hole
with the walls closing in
and the ceiling closing in
I can't breathe
I can't breathe
my clothes reek of petrol
so does my skin
because there's no place to take a shower
all the beer is gone
I drank it all
and all the wine and the vodka
and the Chivas Regal
it's all gone
O black betty bam a lam
Martha threw me out like a used jam rag
I said Martha threw me out like a used jam rag
and now I'm dying
dying
dying
oh yeah she threw me out like a used jam rag
and now I'm dead

The angels will ask me: Was she ambitious? - she was - she wanted to be a screenwriter - She had a falling-apart red spiral notepad she carried around in her purse - we'd be walking around the East Village and she'd whip it out and jot down ideas for movies: there was one about Christ coming back as a white-trash trailer-park girl with super powers - she wants to save the world with her message of love but ends up triggering WW3 - I told her it would make a good animated feature but no no no Amelia had her heart set on a blockbuster starring Linda Hamilton and Rutger Hauer with Sean Penn in a special cameo appearance as the Holy Ghost - at one point she actually enrolled in a screenwriting class - I don't think she ever went or if she did she only went once - the day before her funeral I was walking up 1st Ave. when I heard someone shout my name - I looked across the street - there was this short bald man jumping up and down waving frantically to me with his crash helmet - Timur? Was it Timur Jerk? - I wasn't sure for a second because his head was completely shaved and he was wearing a very expensive-looking red-and-black leather cycle jacket - but yes it *was* Timur - I hadn't seen him or indeed any of the former Cum Jerks in many months - behind him a tall girl was chaining a big motorbike up to the railings outside the Polish diner - Timur came running across the street: Jarleth! Where the fuck you been hiding you fuck? You fuck! You fuck! - I braced myself for the inevitable pummelling - You fuck! You fuck! - The tall girl followed him over - she had blonde pigtails and Nordic freckles and big sad eyes - Prenagass dissis Vera - Vera dissis Prenagass from Dublin - so we stood there in the cold and chatted about old times - how's so-and-so - have you seen so-and-so - everybody was in rehab - in the middle of regaling me with an account of accident-prone Charles's latest mishap (a fall while roofing) Timur lowered his voice and said Hey listen about tomorrow if you need a ride we're all going out in the van - Thanks I said I don't - So you got a ride? - No I said I'm not going - You're not going? Waddaya mean you're not going? - I mean I'm not going I said - Timur stared at me hard but he said nothing - Vera put her hand on his arm - he shook it off and abruptly walked back across the street - he started kicking the railings outside the Polish place and swearing in what I suppose was Ukrainian - some school children stopped to stare - Vera said: He's upset. He assumed - I know I said. I'm sorry. Tell him I'm sorry. I've given it a lot of thought. I can't go to the funeral. It's the thought of her lying in that coffin - Yes she said. Coffins are so small - across the street Timur had unchained the bike and was pointedly gunning the engine - he bellowed VERA! CUMAWN! - Vera and I shook hands gravely - then she turned and walked away - nice long legs nice small bum blonde pigtails bobbing sadly in the breeze - a minute later they roared past me - I saluted them with my hip flask - Vera waved - Timur eyes front jaw clenched gave me the finger - and to think we used to do pints of Robatussin together

---

here lies

AMELIA JANE FRANCESCA GARRITY

a.k.a.

'Your little white whore'

1968(?) - 1993

STRIPPER - THIEF - JUNKIE - SUICIDE

we are put on earth a little space

that we may learn to bear the beams of love

Wm. Blake

JOHN PAUL GEORGE RINGO COME ON LADS ALL TOGETHER
NOW

we all live in a charnel house of fear
a charnel house of fear
a charnel house of fear

we all live in a charnel house of fear
a charnel house of fear
a charnel house of fear

and our friends have bloodstained hands
many more of them have swollen glands
and the band begins to play

the Leather Nun was here
but left

Bone stuck in throat

K'AN

The watery depths are twofold.

Have faith.

He keeps his heart faithful and prospers.

Whatever he does is worthwhile.

Line 1: The waters are twofold.

The man enters the watery cavern.

There is evil.

XMAS EVE

Sean there IS evil - you never said a truer word

You're probably not familiar with the I-Ching - a handy way of deciding what to do next invented by our friends the ching-chong Chinamen in days of yore and still v. popular today with bohos and hippie burnouts - Personally I've always thought Eastern mysticism was a load of bollocks - of course Martha was into it we had frequent rows about crystals runes astrology all that New Age twaddle - ditto Raptor: many's the time she tried to drag me to spook sessions on the upr. east side - old chicks in leotards frothing at the mouth calling up the souls of ancient Celtic warriors - are you there Finglas MacBray? Show yourself Strong Thighs! - No thank YOU - Prendy's Creed: I accept that the curse laid upon me by the Young Witch of Trim on the night of the 8th of September 1983 is a real and terrible fact - all the rest = bullshit and fakery - but - BIG proviso - after THE BIRCHMONT REVELATION (which we'll get to in a minute) I have to be open to anything that might hasten the successful completion of OPERATION SNUFFOUT - I was messing about on Vincent's computer just now and by accident (or was it??) I found the I-Ching (under 'GAMES') - I thought all right nothing ventured nothing gained so I typed in my question:

HOW SHALL I KILL LE FROG?

Up popped the hexagram K'AN - 'The man enters the watery cavern' - I immediately got a flash of Holmes and Moriarty locked in their famous death embrace high above the roar and spray of the Ruggerbugger Falls - Then I asked it

WILL I GET AWAY WITH IT?

and it gave me K'AN again - so you see all in all I'm greatly encouraged

I see Sean scratching his head: 'Birchmont Revelation? Le Frog? Get away with *what?*' - The fact is dear shade there have been some major developments since we last communed - sorry I've been off the radar: I needed to take a break and screw the old head back on - things got a bit out of hand back in November - the boozing got out of hand - my poor old nerves went belly-up - black clouds descended: I became exceedingly morose brooding on Amelia / Martha / my homeless crisis / being cheated by the aunts etc. - I'm happy to report I've snapped back 100% - I'm fit and working again which is just as it should be because *there's a serious job of work to be done*

I'm not living in the garage any more - That whole scene got busted - Olegarkis had a spy on the street: an old VFW guy called Buddy started snooping around late at night and in the end despite my best efforts to get on his good side the old fuck blew the whistle on me - on the morning of Dec. 6th my studio was raided by Christos and the Brothers O. - 5:30 A.M.: I was fast asleep - they burst in - you should have seen them - terrible hysterical carry-on / typical Mediterranean overreaction - shouting cursing knocking things over - they brought a PITBULL Sean - the fucking thing nearly took my hand off - Alex Olegarkis was standing over me shining a flashlight in my eyes the other brother Georgie was swinging a baseball bat - all 3 of them yelling at me and the dog growling and snapping - you'd think I was the head of a South American drug cartel not some poor sod trying to keep a roof over his head after his wife kicked him out - Upshot: I was thrown out on the street w/ my few belongings

– luckily I had Mr. Cherry Red on me – alarmed by a strange noise I'd shoved him down my boot the night before and they never saw him – of course THEY'RE extremely lucky I didn't lose my head and start blasting – instead I stood by calmly and watched Georgie beat the crap out of my boombox – I was informed that I'd have my legs broken if they ever caught me within a mile of the property - then the 3 brave brothers piled into their pick-up with the pitbull and took off in the direction of the BQE - Chris at the wheel fat Georgie smirking and sinister Alex waving back at me - I crashed at Ken's for 3 days - Maude was away visiting family in Detroit – I spent the next week at the Bowery Mission (the food's quite good and the conversation's excellent) – they don't like their guests toting gats so Privette had to hold my .38 – it took a lot of coaxing and pleading I never knew he was such a nervous nelly - I spent the next 4 days with Raptor - a shameful caving in I know but I was desperate - I paid for it Sean: between the smell of cat piss and the damn parrot squawking and Raptor's cheerful whistling I nearly went mad - I can still hear the drone of the blender: Here you are Jarleth I've made you yet ANOTHER nourishing pint of celery-beet juice - I'd pretend to drink it but I spat it out in the plant pot when she wasn't looking - to add to my punishment she made me watch the Riverdance video with her at least 500 times - bang thump bang wallop - NA nega na nega na nega nega na - at one point I hallucinated I was a rhinestone on Flatley's headband - I tried to console myself with visions of Roman arenas full of crucified teddy bears the little fuckers impaled and in flames and yours truly dancing like Nero w/ a burning brand howling with glee I'm a Firestarter a twisted Firestarter - 4 days with Raptor Sean was my absolute limit - after I quit her Bower of Bliss I spent the night in a doorway on lower Broadway - nothing between me and the cold east wind but a sleeping bag 2 flattened cardboard boxes and a thermos flask of Georgi vodka - in fitful dreams moaning and shivering I passed the night en plein air - I woke up in a black depression - I couldn't face Vincent and the zombies so I called in sick - I spent the afternoon at the Blue and Gold playing pool and drinking with some prep school potheads I met outside Gem Spa - 3 likable upper crust truants named Biff and Brent and Boo - Boo especially was a bottomless well of cash - We emptied pitcher after pitcher of Bass toasting Great Irishmen of the Past William S. Burroughs James Joyce The Pogues our furious orgy of mug clinking punctuated by trips outside to smoke a spliff - With dusk approaching I said goodbye to my 3 young friends and wandered west - I had a vague idea I'd check out the Max Beckman show at the downtown Gug however on a Prendian whim I veered south instead and in a restaurant on either Thompson or Sullivan I met charming Stephanie - an inch maybe 2 under 6 foot - legs without end - c. 23-25 - auburn tresses - she was drunk so was I - we hit it off immediately - sloshed as she was I noticed she had good posture and a mischievous twinkle in her eye - I caught a hint that she might be up for some horizontal gymnastics later on - after c. 10 min. chatting I told her I knew a place that wasn't so crowded - she said all right - bye bye to her 2 girlfriends who looked far from pleased by this development - I remember walking down the street with my arm around her neck - cream raincoat yellow wool scarf sensible shoes she was the Compleat Office Temp - we dived into a little place somewhere in Little Italy where I ordered a bucket of squid and some more red wine - So what do you do to keep the wolf from the door Stephanie? - I'm a legal secretary but I study Caribbean dance 2 nights a week - Fair fucks to you Stephanie - And what do YOU do? - I'm an experimental filmmaker - Wow. Did you make movies back in Ireland? That's where you're from right? - That is where I'm from. Movies? Tons of them. In actual fact I'm one of the founding fathers of the Irish film industry - Wow. Do you know . . . Neil Jordan? - Do I know Neil Jordan! Course I know Neil me and Neil go way back. We made art flicks together in the '70s at Rathmines Tech. I was the ideas man he followed me around manning the hash pipe - Have you seen *Dracula*? - Not yet - It's great. I love Tom Cruise. Do you like Tom Cruise? - Oh sure Tom's . . . fab (bite the bullet Prendy she has world-class buzzumbas) - Listen Stephanie would you like to sleep with me? - I don't know. Would I? - the coy maid - I think you would - Maybe. I don't know - Pause - She: Hey would you like to go to a PARTY? - Yeah sure - the only thing is it's up in Westchester - Westchester! I thought you meant party at your place. Who's having the party? - My boss - Your boss. What do you do again? - I'm a legal secretary - Oh yes so your boss is a lawyer? - Yes and you really have to meet him - hmmm well to tell you the truth I'm very down on lawyers at the moment. Not a lot of respect for that profession - Oh but you'll like my boss. He's very charming. He's also very rich and he loves movies - Loves movies? Is that a fact? - immediately the INVESTOR light went on in my head - Well what the fuck are we waiting for! Knock that back Steph and let's get out of here!

We got a taxi to Grand Central and hopped on Metro North - I don't remember the actual train ride but I do remember getting into some sort of altercation with the taxi driver who drove us from the station - Stephanie paid the fare and the next thing I knew we were in this brightly lit hallway marble floor pillars huge urns stuffed with tropical plants a big sweeping staircase cream walls under huge chandeliers - I decided on the spot to ask Stephanie's boss for $100,000 and let him talk me down to $70,000. A tiny I'm sure shamefully exploited Mexican maid took our coats - I refused to surrender my Cum Jerks cap - we strolled into the party room - it was crammed floor to ceiling with well heeled punters - $2000 suits evening gowns gold tie pins pearls diamonds Rolex watches etc. - typical cocktail party buzz / hum / chatter - drunk as I was it hit me this might be Celeb City - the next second I spotted Kate Moss and Naomi Campbell over in a corner talking to this black guy - it wasn't them as it turned out - everybody was yapping away at 100 m.p.h. nobody listening - 3 or 4 sullen-looking kids in tuxes were circling with trays of nibbles and tall glasses of the bubblesome refresher - I snagged 2 for me and Stephanie downed both instanto and snagged 2 more from another serf drifting the other way - I also grabbed a fistful of those little burnt sausages on sticks - So Stephanie I said point out your boss - I can't she said I don't see him anywhere - The next second somebody grabbed her from behind - Ooh - ! - Welcome! - I spun around ready to protect and defend - I saw a tall bloke c. 50-55 jock build west coast tan Armani suit grey hair big white teeth bushy eyebrows - grinning a smoothie-tooth grin - this had to be Mr. $$$$$$ Mine Host - completely ignoring me he turned to a stocky guy beside him: Dan this is Stephanie Hill. Stephanie this is Dan Gelbin. Stephanie is my life support at the office. I cannot live without her and she knows it - hollow booming laugh - Stephanie I'm so glad you could come - he gave her an over-long kiss on the cheek - all Prendergast got was a half second flash of teeth and a curt nod - Enjoy! - and with that Mine Host turned and walked away - I was extremely pissed off because I was all wound up for my introduction: 'Mr. Generous Patron this is Jarleth Prendergast the noted Irish filmmaker' - You see Sean I was very drunk and totally into the idea of getting this fat cat to bankroll SEMTEX / GUMBY / YOUNG WITCH OF TRIM / all my cine-children - The question was should I go after him now or wait until the crowd thinned out a bit? - Better wait I thought - Attorney Moneybags & I would share an intimate brandy sniffing moment in The Den later on - So that was the big boss was it? I said - oh I'm sorry! I didn't introduce you - That's quite all right. What's his name? - Mr. Forvoe - Spell that - F-O-R-V-E-A-U-X - ah a frog! I

thought he had an accent - Yes he's French - Bien. Listen mon vieux
let's not beat around the bush we're both men of the world and busy
bastards. I need $3,000,000 to get MR. SEMTEX up and running
and I want to let you in on the ground floor - you drive a hard bargain
Monsieur Prendergast but I like zee cut of your ghib so why not make
it 6?- Done! - They shake hands and sniff more brandy - that would
be the scene later on: right now I meant to get nice and loose in the
good old holiday spirit - I grabbed some more champers and sausages
- everything was cool: in a while I'd coax Steph upstairs for a quickie
in one of the 50 master bedrooms - But just then I saw the string
quartet - they were jammed into a corner at the far end of the room
- you had to really strain your ears to hear them over the chatter
- I wanted to go over and check them out but I suddenly felt dizzy
- I remember Stephanie saying you're white you're swaying maybe
you should sit down - Yes maybe I should - I let her lead me through
the crush to a big red couch near the back wall - There was no room
to actually sit - it was all couples - so I plonked down on the arm
with my back against the piano - after a minute I felt a bit better -
Where's my drink? I asked her - Stephanie pointed behind me - she'd
set my glass down on the piano which she probably shouldn't have
considering the acidity of champagne but she was totally smashed
herself and didn't care tuppence for the care of fine wood - I'm going
to have a pee she said - have one for me I said winking weakly - she
disappeared - I turned to grab my glass and lo and behold there
was Amelia smiling up at me out of a big gold frame - I was terribly
afraid Sean - I thought I'd lost my mind - I stared at her for God
knows how long - then I reached over and picked it up - it really was
a photograph of Amelia - she was much younger - she looked about
15 - she was wearing blue eyeshadow and her hair was cut short - a
teen Amelia smiling faintly in a gray turleneck sweater - with little
pearl earrings - staring at her I sobered up - not completely but about

90% just like they say you do when you get a shock - my heart was churning - I felt like I'd walked into an electric shower stall and the Untersturmführer-lavatory attendant hit the switch and a million red-hot needle jets of adrenaline blasted out of the showerhead and all the vodka and beer and pot and wine and champers were flushed out of my brainpan - Why is Amelia's picture on the piano? Whose house is this? What am I doing here? Where's Stephanie? - Somebody pinched my hand - I looked down - a tiny creature in pink chiffon with painted-on eyebrows was leering up at me - instinctively I shrank back but the apparition held my sleeve in a grip of iron - the old crone motioned me to bend - I fought to stay erect Sean I fought like mad but her eyes were like black magnets pulling me down - I bent with a shudder into a choking sweet cloud of old lady powder and scent - she cupped a liver-spotted hand to my ear and whispered: I saw you looking at her picture - she nodded at the piano - Did you know her? - I shook my head (Deny Everything) - She whispered: That's Yvonne. She committed suicide. Her poor mother's never got over it. It was a terrible blow to the Birchmont community a terrible blow - I looked back at the picture - Yvonne? No it wasn't. It was Amelia beyond a shadow of a doubt - the old woman was clearly mad - I was about to tell her that but she pointed a long red fingernail: Look! - I looked: there was Mine Host Mr. Suave Sophisto laughing and joking with some guesties not 10 ft. away - So kind so charming she continued. And underneath his poor heart must be broken - Broken? I said. Why broken? - Oh she said her black eyes widening Because he loved her as his own! She was his stepdaughter but he loved her as his own . . . Tragic . . . Tragic . . . and shaking her head she let go of my sleeve and the crowd swallowed her up - I remember thinking: I've wandered into hell - it's a simple mistake - I'll walk out into the hall the maid will give me back my coat I'll walk out the front door and an angelic policeman will escort me back to Earth - I looked across the room - Mr. Grieving Stepdad had vanished - I stood in the midst of the noisome throng Sean willing myself to wake up - WAKE UP PRENDERGAST IT'S TIME - Suddenly Stephanie popped up in front of me: Here you are! Are you feeling better? God! What's the matter? - Life Stephanie life - You look terrible - I've had a bit of a shock - She took my paw: Come into the other room - I snatched it back - She said: What's the matter? You wanted to meet my boss - I must have looked at her blankly - Mr. Forveaux. Pierre my boss? - Pierre your boss - Pierre ? - Yes but everybody calls him Peter—

The next thing I remember I was shouldering my way through the crush of pampered bodies peering this way and that my head revolving 360 - Where are you Peter where did you go? you were here a minute ago - thou villain I was thinking - thou something something string of adjectives from *Hamlet* villain

Thou *smiling* villain

For lo Sean the penny had dropped the spark had jumped the gap:

Pierre the Boss = Peter the Rapist

Evil Peter - Peter whose cock she choked on - Peter who fucked her up the ass - you made my best girl cry you fuck

My heart was pounding - I felt like the Greek of old tricked into eating his kiddies at the feast - I wanted to disgorge with all violence - I'd drunk the bastard's booze I'd eaten his disgusting little burnt sausages - My head was spinning - You lied to me Amelia or Yvonne or whatever your name is - you said you were raped by a friend of the family - and all the time it was your stepfather???? - hang on: if

Peter's her stepfather who's Dan Garrity? - and what about Eileen the sainted mom and sister Patty? - this isn't blue-collar Inwood this is Birchmont The Cream of Westchester home of the big bucks - I'm telling you Sean basic models of reality were crashing all around me like century-old redwoods - I was drowning - at the same time I was shouldering my way through the crowd - Scuse - scuse me - coming through - gang way you pack of locusts - Stephanie was back there somewhere lost in the sea of bodies - eons slid by - eventually I fell out into the hall - it was completely deserted - where are you Peter? - either he was still in the party room or he was in another room - or - quite likely - he was upstairs having his way with Stephanie! - I stood at the foot of the big stairs trying to get my bearings - I knew I had to pull myself together / gather my wits - I was patting my pockets looking for my fags when I saw the little Mexican maid - she was standing by the front door holding my coat - it was very eerie - how did she know I was coming out right at that moment? - she stood there in silence regarding me calmly from behind that moon-round face of stone - I walked over to her - I let her help me into my coat - I was calm I was rational - she opened the big front door - Buenas noches señor - Buenas noches - I began to exit - but I changed my mind - I turned around took a deep breath squared my shoulders and started walking back into the party room - I'd decided to kill him right there and then Sean - in preparation I took my coat off and flung it from me - as luck would have it the stupid thing struck a huge antique vase and knocked it off its plinth SSSMAAAASSSH!!!!! - coo Prendy you've done it now - I bent over to pluck my coat from the pot shards - then I swung around and pointed at the maid: Your boss - su patrone - es un muy malo hombre. Leave this house of sin mi niña you are free to go - at that moment 2 big jock types in tuxes came down the stairs - they saw the vase - they saw Prendy - Hey! What's going on? barked the bigger one - of course I must have had GATECRASHER written all over me - anyway polo club nods were exchanged and they both came at me - but in the blink of an eye Prendy had bounded down the front steps - another blink and I was legging it down the long floodlit gravel drive crunch crunch crunch in the direction of the front gates - I ran out into the road - totally out of puff I put on the brakes about 300 yds from the house - for a long time Sean I stood there panting and glaring back at the faux-old-world towers of the sorcerer's mansion - then I launched into a Berserker War Dance a stomping clodhopper from the dawn of time - oh how I danced! - as I stomped and leapt and slid and twirled I swore Vengeance upon Pierre Forveaux - I swore him whacked - I swore I'd put him in his coffin and do a jig on the lid - Renvanche! Renvanche! - my arms were flailing I was laughing hysterically and I don't mind telling you I even shat a little in my pants as I danced danced danced - I don't know how long I kept it up but when I finally collapsed in the road I was wheezing and sweating like a pig - For the next hour I wandered the residential backroads of Birchmont looking for the train station - I found it at last and got the last train back to the city - I ask you to picture me slumped in my seat in that almost empty carriage sucking on a fag in open breach of Metro North regulations staring out the window at the cold starless night - you can never know the mountain of misgivings I was having - My God Sean I'd left that nice young girl behind - I'd abandoned Stephanie to the hot breath and sweaty hands of an Armani-suited necromancer - All the way back to Grand Central I had to keep reminding myself that I'd done the right thing i.e. I was right to split when I did - no point confronting Le Frog on his home turf no point at all - those upper class tough boy kinsmen of his would have chucked me down the front steps in a second and kicked the shit out of me - No instead I'd been very smart and canny: by tactically retreating rather than attacking like the proverbial wounded bull I've gained immeasurably on the stealth front - now it's *my* move - I know his last name - plus I know (more or less) where he lives - it just goes to show: you can spend years and years in some smokey forest grotto sacrificing bats and mice to Father Odin and have absolutely nothing to show for it and then suddenly out of the clear blue The Norns give you a BONUS REPLAY - now it's all up to Jarleth L. Prendergast Secret Agent of Vengeance and democratically elected leader of the lynch mob - Sean Reynolds come and stand beside me - fill your ghostly lungs with what passes for air in those sad cypress groves where you wander beyond The Shimmering Veil - let our war cry ring out across the rooftops of fabled high-towered Manhattan - the bat signal is up and

OPERATION SNUFFOUT IS GO

———·———

XMAS MORNING 6 A.M.

here lies
YVONNE FORVEAUX
a.k.a.
AMELIA JANE FRANCESCA GARRITY

We are put on earth a little space
to make a fool out of Jarleth Prendergast

———·———

Children - Shall I tell you a fairy story? A fairy story for Xmas?

Oh yes Mary Poppins! Please yes a fairy story!

Once upon a time in Inwood New York there lived an unhappy little girl named Amelia Jane Francesca Garrulosity - Born in the year of grace 19686970 she grew up blue collar Irish Catholic - Amelia was 4 when her sainted mother Eileen The Flesh Eating Shamrock died in childspawn leaving Amelia and wee sister Pimples to cope with The Da a vicious psycho pisspot who beat his 2 daughters every night with a huge caveman club studded with rusty nails and barbed wire and then with gallons of innocent child's blood trickling down the walls Dan would plonk down in his lazee boy and toss off 50 double shots of Bushmills one after the other and sit there blubbering over old snapshots of Eileen the Dead Shamrock Mommy - after a while Dan would blow chunks and go to the bathroom in his troors and curse St. Patrick for a fairy coachman and scream - scream Dan scream - scream and cuss bang your big hairy paws on the table - for the grand finale he jumps up on a plastic Connemara pony and they gallop off into the Keltic Sunset - My God Sean what a twisted web she wove! And how completely I was taken in!! - Fast-talking Prendy who's been known to bend the truth and insert a yam *how totally and utterly I fell for her jive!!* - it was all lies Sean - all that stuff about Dan the tyrannical da and the nightly thrashings! Lies! Lies! Lies! There was never any such person as Amelia Garrity or Dan Garrity or Eileen the mommy-saint or little sister Patty! - It was all a patchwork quilt of shameless fibs and worn out Irish-American clichés!!! - in reality Yvonne Forveaux grew up in upper upper UPPER class Birchmont wanting for nothing: I'm sure she had a horse and a Jeep Cherokee and holidays in the S. of France and jetskis ballet lessons a cool Toshiba sound system wardrobes overflowing with cool designer teen clothing plus a pupil of a pupil of Rimsky-Korsikov would come to the house once a week to show her how to rock the 88s - it's laughable really when I think about how I used to picture Dan the Da sitting in their pokey little '70s kitchenette in Inwood in his Con Ed overalls sleeves rolled up fat white hairy arms grey sideburns five o'clock shadow the bottle on the table self-pity blazing in his eyes - HOW WAS I TO KNOW HE WAS ONLY A FIGMENT OF HER SICK IMAGINATION? Sean Reynolds raises his hand: 'But it makes no sense. Why would a Daughter of $$$$$$ and Westchester Privilege pretend to be a working-class Irish-American Supervixen?' - I honestly don't know Sean - I'm not a family therapist - I suppose she didn't like her life (duh!) - after she bust out of Birchmont Maximum Security Prison for Spoilt Rich Kids and hit the Big City she invented Amelia Garrity - thinking back she didn't look Irish at all - wrong complexion etc.- of course she was acting in a grand tradition: New York's always been about ambitious out-of-towners reinventing themselves - Sean: 'But the girl was a pathological liar!' - I'd have to agree - 'Well then - how can you possibly believe her story about being raped?' - good question - all I know is this: if you'd seen her that night if you'd heard her voice you wouldn't have any doubts - everything she said he did he did - so much so that on a night in December in the toilet on the 4th or 5th floor of a seedy women's hotel up on West 48th St. well-known scene-shaker / tough rock 'n' roll chick Amelia Garrity took a dressing gown chord and made a running knot in it - she climbed up on the bath and tied one end to an overhead pipe - she slipped the noose around her neck - Pierre or Peter her stepfather was standing in the shadows smiling and egging her on: 'You're worthless Yvonne you're a fuck-up you only have yourself to blame you're disgusting diseased a hooker and a junkie I wouldn't touch you now - no I wouldn't touch you with a 10 ft pole' etc. - on and on he droned he wouldn't stop so to shut him up she stepped off the side of the bath - eyes popping fingers scrabbling frantically at the knot piss running down her leg jerking and twitching and then no more fight just swinging to and fro - in a few minutes all the years of self-disgust and humiliation were choked off - and now she's down in hell in whatever circle it is with all the other self-slaughtering cats and kitties and he drove her to it but by the Norns' good graces I've found the bastard and it's time for The BIG Payback - Let me put it to you this way: remember the end of *The Maltese Falcon* Sean? - when Bogey's trying to explain to Mary Astor why he has to shop her for killing Miles Archer? - 'You see sc'weetheart when your partner gets killed you're supposed to do something about it. If you don't do something well it's bad for business etc. etc.' - it's a great piece of dialogue I used to have it memorised - Here's the point: Pierre Forveaux killed MY partner and now I have to do something about it - you can argue till you're blue in the face that he didn't actually literally 'kill' her - to me that's just a silly legalism - he killed her Sean - he killed her with contempt - and now out of the clear blue I've been given a chance to nail him - if I don't make the absolute most of this why I may as well turn in my .38 quit being a private detective and go off somewhere and open up a little gas station - but you know it wouldn't work because sooner or later The Past always comes knocking - I dig you daddy says Sean I dig you - and the deaf mute kid looks up slowly from gutting a fish and smiles

---

COMMAND POST / XMAS DAY 2 P.M.

Command Post? says Sean furrowing his spectral brows - Command Post? What's all this? - Excerpt from *New York* magazine article that will never be written:

'By day an ineptly managed West Village copy shop, by night Vincent's Kwik Copy is magically transformed into The Amelia Jane Francesca Garrity-Yvonne Forveaux Memorial Command Post. The Command Post is staffed by Agents of the Committee to Exterminate Pierre "Peter" Forveaux, Attorney-at-Law. The Post's Operations Manager and the Chief Coordinator of OPERATION SNUFFOUT and

OPERATION SNUFFOUT PHASE ONE: PROJECT STALKER
is Jarleth L. Prendergast. A serious-minded articulate man from
the Emerald Isle, Prendergast is a noted experimental filmmaker
in his own right . . .'

As CPs go Kwik is a vast improvement on my Williamsburg studio - I moved in the night before last (Xmas Eve Eve) - it was the
ideal time to do it - no zombies around because of the holidays and
Vincent the boss down in Key West - It goes without saying that
what I'm doing is totally illegal - how I got keys I won't go into
- Command Post Rule Number One: *never* turn the lights on in the
front because people can see in from the street - Vincent's office
(because it's at the back) is the hub of the action / the Command
Post's Nerve Centre or Center - last night I got settled in: my holiday
bottle of Johnny Walker Red Label is tucked away at the bottom
of a filing cab - the gun formerly known as Mr. Cherry Red - I
rechristened him McSplatter - is safe in his new special secret
hiding place - all my gear / my sleeping bag etc. is hidden in the
back storeroom where we keep the drums of toner - last night I
started compiling the DOSSIER ON THE ACCUSED on Vincent's
Mac - I packed it in around 3:30 drank a toast to Satan (I'm reading Baudelaire again) and crashed on the couch - Vincent's couch
in contrast to Ken's is loooooong and wide and v. comfy - I've got
a computer and a chair - there's a little fridge for my bevvies - all
in all it's not a bad set-up at all: I'm ready ready ted to rock 'n'
roll i.e. to kick-start PROJECT STALKER - I've given it a lot of
thought Sean: when you're out to whack a rich cat like Forveaux
AND GET AWAY WITH IT you don't have a prayer unless you
zero in on him *outside* his fortress-compound - at first I thought
a commando-style raid on the Birchmont mansion might do it: 3
A.M. Prendy crawls across the manicured lawn in blackface black

poloneck black slacks black gloves wire cutters grappling hooks
drugged meat for the dogs - he rappels down from the roof onto the
little balcony outside the master bedroom like the chap in the old
Milk Tray ads except I wouldn't be dropping off a box of chocs for
my lady fair I'd be there to plug an archvillain in the goolies - after
weighing the pros and cons I rejected this Delta Force Night Raid
scenario - too many variables - next I thought CAR AMBUSH and
was filled with boiling rage because I don't have a car - By God and
the Great Whore of Babylon if I ever needed a cash fuel injection
it's NOW - I've a good mind to ring up McGrath and shout at him
just for the hell of it - hey fuck-head here's the latest: I'm out to
make the world a better place by executing one of YOUR lousy
profession - Dick the Butcher gimme 5! - meanwhile I live in fear
knowing that Forveaux could chopper off to an attack-proof island
stronghold in Micronesia at any moment - I'm talking Sean about
an island so well guarded by electrified robosharks / machine-gun
nests / cyborg bodyguards that not even a Legion of the Damned
Style Swat Team led by Steven Seagal Claude Van Dam Wesley
Snipes Bruce Willis Sean Connery and Ice Cube could put a dent
in it - In other words time is tight: I have to execute Le Frog SOON
before he slips through the dragnet

OK here's what PROJECT STALKER looks like:
1. Find out what law firm he's with
2. put a tail on him
3. build detailed profile of his daily routine and contacts
4. infiltrate the workplace for intelligence gathering
5. establish a 5th column
6. possible use of sophisticated surveillance equipment (budget
permitting)

Dec. 25th: 4:30 P.M.

PROJECT STALKER: my 1st task is to find out where Peter works
i.e. which of the million and one Gotham law firms he's with - nail that
down and I've got a possible execution site or at least a known point
where he shows up and leaves from 5 days a week (???) - mon homme
de loi lives in Birchmont ergo he's probably a partner in a swanky
Manhattan outfit - but not necessarily!! - Vincent has the Manhattan
Brooklyn Bronx & Queens Yellow Pages plus the Westchester and
NJ but not the CT or Staten Is. ones so you can see right away I'm
stymied by gaping holes in the infomatrix - on top of which the YPs
don't list lawyers alphabetically - that would be too easy!!!! - No they're
listed 'By Practice' - so I'm having to wade through ACCIDENT- PER-
SONAL INJURY - PROPERTY DAMAGE - ADMINISTRATIVE
- AVIATION - BANKRUPTCY - CIVIL RIGHTS - COMMERCIAL
- CRIMINAL - FAMILY . . . and so on and so on - 60 shagging pages
in the Manhattan one alone - so far I've found 2 firms with a partner
named Forveaux: 1 in Manhattan 1 in Brooklyn - I called the one at
768 Broadway: Hartley Forveaux and something - of course there was
nobody there - the message said have a happy and peaceful holiday
season and call back after the 1st - it's tragic Sean: here I am chomp-
ing at the bit eager to stalk eager to whack but I'm paralysed by this
grotesque parody of a Christian holiday - I say bring back the Roman
Saturnalia - break out the togas and sandals the slave shall tweak the
master's nose with impunity etc.- it's high time we took all this Away
In A Manger Silent Night sleighbells in the snow Mr. Pickwick and
his friends crap and swept it into the sulfurous pit and screwed down
the lid - when I was a kid I loved Xmas but now I fucking hate it - it's
forever tainted: you have to remember the week before the Lamb o'
God Monster Blowout was when Amelia offed herself

—————•—————

COMMAND POST / XMAS NIGHT: I was in shock but that's no excuse: exiting the Forveaux mansion without Stephanie's phone number was an act of criminal stupidity - not only is she One Hot Temp she's also a crucially important link to HIM - and I let her get away!! - *I don't know her last name* - I dimly recall he called her Stephanie Hill - I spent a good portion of yesterday and today calling or trying to call all the Stephanie Hills and S. Hills in the tristate area - by the hokeys I'm keeping those 411 wallahs busy! - No joy as yet - if I exhaust the Hills I'll turn to the S. Halls and Stephanie Halls S. Howells and S. Hales and S. Yules and S. Lyles - and after that? Fan out and quiz all the Hubbles Heinzes Hendersons Hicks Hogans and Herschs?? - I don't know Sean I really don't - Not only is OPERATION FIND-STEPH proving incredibly time consuming it's also quite dangerous because these are paranoid times: everybody's star-69 crazy - I've had people hang up on me and then call back and leave messages on the answering machine here complaining that their privacy's been violated that I spoilt their Xmas dinner I woke little Suzie up from her nap etc. - One man - a Mr. S. Hill of the Bronx - threatened to have me 'deported back to England you nosey limey cocksucker' - To protect the Command Post I've had to erase the 'Hello you've reached Vincent's Kwik Copy' greeting - which reminds me I have to rerecord it tonight because they're all back tomorrow - Peggy Pam Meshell Yung Keith Robbie the Robot Alice Daisy Deepak Laverne Jesus Mimi Brian = the Gen X Slacker Battalion / Mad Vincent's Zombie Horde - this time tomorrow they'll be swarming all over the gaff banging around in their designer lumberjack boots jacked into retro rubbish on their Walkmans rehearsing their silly hiphop routines shake it don't break it it took your mother 9 months to make it and generally violating the sanctity of the Command Post - for the sake of the mission I must stay strong and focused

Dec. 26th: BOXING DAY 5:30 A.M. - re FINDSTEPH I'm forced to the conclusion that either (a) she's unlisted (b) she doesn't have a phone (unlikely!?) or (c) she has a phone but it's not in her name - I'll have to put an ad in the *Voice* personals HELLO STEPHANIE REMEM-BER ME? SEXY IRISH FILM GUY. I'D REALLY LIKE TO SEE YOU AGAIN - last night I popped my head into several Italian joints including Bastiani's on Thompson St. which I'm almost 100% sure is where we met: no sign of her or the 2 girlfriends (one was super-skinny with a big conk the other was a short chubby blonde with fat ankles) - Actually I'd have been v. surprised if she was around: I bet you anything she's out of town visiting her parents in Wallawocka-wumpa Indiana or whatever she's from - STEPHANIE IF YOU'RE OUT THERE EATING LEFTOVER TURKEY IF YOU CAN HEAR ME FOLLOW THE SOUND OF MY VOICE RIDE MUSIC BEAM BACK TO BASE

DEC 26: COMMAND POST OVERRUN!!

How was your holiday? - It sucked man - How was yours? - It sucked - yes Sean my co-workers are back - colourfully attired and sporting a collective IQ of 300 the gang's all here: Yung - who's actually quite intelligent I don't know how he got stuck at Kwik - is handing around Polaroids of his 2 month old son - Here's Meshell A.K.A. the Queen of Sheba inscrutable hot and haughty and completely ignoring me as usual - if you're so cool Meshell how come your musical horizons stop at Janet Jackson?- I tell ya Shaolin Temple Guards are def and phat my sista - word - Here's Keith the gentle giant of Kwik gazing out the window stoned out of his gourd as usual his eyes all red and puffy - any good news on those Thai sticks Keith? - a stoic shake of the huge head - meanwhile from the boss's office (*my* office!!!) comes the unmistakable nicotine-coated rasp of our beloved employer and spiritual father Vincent Szabo - Vincent's on the blower threatening to report a paper supplier to the Better Business Bureau - my co-worker Alice Worth shoulders past me scowling her scowl - Alice is an artist she lives with 115 cats and makes hairball sculptures - Meanwhile Jesus is telling Pam that he dreams about her every night and would relish the opportunity of giving her a series of brain-stopping orgasms - I can take you there girl - oh yeah? - Afterwards though forget it you have to go be a nun - Pam giggles coyly Alice pushes past me again and for the millionth time I ask will night never come?

12/27: ASSAULT ON COMMAND POST: RAPTOR AT 4 O'CLOCK: it happened at lunch time - I was just nipping out for my slice of Sicilian when suddenly there she was in my face like a fucking jack-in-the-box blocking the doorway: Jarleth where have you been? - now now Gwyneth calm yourself - cool and collected I grabbed Maid Marion by the elbow and started steering her away from Zombie House - she was babbling at a furious rate: Jarleth I called Ken but he didn't return any of my calls so I went around to 5th Street and I knocked and knocked but nobody answered so I waited out on the stoop and when he came home I confronted him. He said you'd left town (good man Privette!) I didn't believe him. I'm really angry with you Jarleth - Angry? Why are you angry? - You broke my television - I did not - You did. You pushed it off the table and sat on it - Keep your voice down Gwyneth. I didn't break your TV - Yes Jarleth you did. It's always the same. You do fucked-up things when you're drunk and then you don't remember - No you're right I don't remember and now if you'll excuse me I have to go to lunch goodbye - How dare you walk away from me! - no response - Bastard! - I kept walking - You're a loser Jarleth! A pathetic loser with delusions of grandeur! - sticks and stones Gwyneth sticks and stones - bad filmmaker! - I whipped around: What did you say? - I said all your films SUCK! - I'm sorry Sean I snapped - I lowered my head and with a terrible roar I charged her - What actually happened was I started the charge but I slipped on the ice - special thanks here to maintenance zombies Keith and Mimi for doing such a splendid job scraping the sidewalk this morning - anyway down I went - thinking back I should have stayed down sued Vincent for negligence and ended my days in peace and comfort in a condo in Miami - instead like a fool I jumped up and went after her - Raptor had vanished - I stood there fuming looking all around - I walked to the corner - No sign of her - Where is she? Where are you? - Raptor! RAPTOR!! - Come back you silly woman I need your credit cards

———•———

12/27 STALKER UPDATE: I just spoke to the receptionist at Ryan Forveaux Wattler (a law practice in Brooklyn Heights) - I inquired very politely if their Mr. Lance Forveaux was by any chance known as Pierre or Peter to his friends - the recept. said no: Lance's official nickname was The Cheesecutter - charming - disengage probe - I have to say I'm being plagued by terrible doubts Sean: what if Forveaux's one of those super-slick free-floating corporate legal consultant high rollers w/out portfolio?? i.e. he's impossible to find because he's not on the mast head of any one firm?? Another possibility: what if he doesn't practice in the tristate area? Flash of stalkee sipping a pernod laptopping away on the D.C. shuttle - Enter Prendy disguised as dining car attendant - I creep up behind him a steak knife concealed under my apron - we enter a tunnel - blackout - gurgle gurgle

———•———

Dec. 27th 10 P.M. - a definite plus about Kwik Living is that Vincent has a VCR - because of the enormous responsibilities I'm shouldering as first officer in charge of the Command Post it's vital that I take time out to relax unwind recharge my batteries etc. - to this end I've decided to make tonight a Blockbuster Night or rather a Killer Bee

Blockbuster Night - in preparation I've tacked my sleeping bag up across the window and jacked in the headphones

KILLER BEE = 3 parts Jägermeister
2 parts Barenjäger
one chilled mug

BLOCKBUSTER = family ent. conglom owned and operated by the Christian Right though I must admit their foreign film section *has* improved over the years - I took 3 flicks out on Raptor's card (she forgot to delete me!!!!) - I intend to spend a few pleasant hours communing with the Killer Bees as I watch and rewatch Godard's CONTEMPT especially that famous scene at the end where Piccoli's stalking Jack Palance through the labyrinth under the Corsican villa - you may recall Sean it's the point where the film finally takes off after hrs of tedious back and forth mais oui ma chérie tu es evidement une femme et pour vous plaire je suis un homme très très malheureaux bullshit between Piccoli and Bardot - at last Palance the Arsehole Big Shot Producer is cornered - we see him as we've wanted to see him all along: i.e. scared shitless sweating trembling pressed against the wall in the shadows like Harry Lime in his tight '60s drip-dry black suit - and here's Piccoli - Retribution Personified - taking careful aim - p't-chooo! - the angry husband slugs go whistling through the air barely missing our Jack to ricochet off the pseudo greek pillars with gorgeous little plaster dust explosions - Palance starts pleading for his life Listen to me Philippe or Jean or whatever your name is you gotta give me a break. I got a brain tumour. You understand? A brain tumour! The doctors give me 2 months to live! Yes! To live! That's why I acted like an asshole. That's why I had a tantrum and threw the silver salver across the screening room. I don't want your wife. You can keep her. Blondes give me indigestion. A wise man once said truly it is better not to have been born. Jean! Claude? Luc? Answer me goddam it! - and all the time the cute brunette

interpreter is translating this astonishing outburst into frog but Piccoli
is unmoved - he stays cool in his porkpie hat - he's closing in now and the
bullets are missing Jacko's head by fractions of millimetres - meanwhile
Fritz Lang is lurking in the shadows polishing his monocle mumbling
quotes from Novalis and Hölderlin and the Brothers Grimm - all at once
Palance utters his famous cry one part rage 2 parts despair and makes
a desperate break for it up the wide stone staircase - Piccoli gives chase
blasting away - then there's the unforgettable cut to Bardot standing
in blazing sunshine her divinely naked bum filling the screen as she
recites a fragment of the *Iliad* to the drooling film crew - What I'm trying to say is that in this despicable Weak-Kneed Age this wishy washy
Timid Time with Psych Central / Crowd Control leaning on us to forgive
those who trespass against us Real Men like Michel Piccoli and myself
refuse to yield - i.e. I don't give a tinker's damn about Forveaux's secret
sorrows - e.g. 'But Mr. Prendergast! Monsieur Forveaux suffers from
autointellectoerectolitis, a potentially fatal disease where the penis
grows a tiny little brain of its own' - No No No No - No biographical tidbit
ever can or ever will negate the fact that a disgusting sex crime has
been perpetrated upon the fragile psyche of an adolescent girl - Amelia
should have grown up to be the mother of a gang of bonny blue-haired
children - my children - only that lecherous bastard couldn't keep his
paws off her - Godard's message is unequivocal: there'll be no peace in
the valley and no peace for Agent Prendergast till Pierre Forveaux is
6ft. under doing his bit for the nitrogen cycle

no

Forveaux

no Forveaux

no Forveaux

is

go

go

go

Dec. 28th: Killer Bee killer hangover this morning but that's what you pay for - It's only a matter of time before I find him: when I nail down where he works the next step is to *infiltrate the work place* for intelligence gathering: Ruse 1 = impersonate a plant waterer - I arrive bright and early at his office in a peaked cap / overalls with a couple of props watering can spray bottle some packets of plant food - Receptionist: 'I'm sorry there must be some mistake. The plant waterer was just here' - Me: 'I know. That was Jim. Jim's Basic Maintenance. I'm McAlpine the photosynthesist.' - Recept: 'I'm sorry?' Me: 'It's OK. It's in your service contract. You get the chlorophyll stim and the photon bombardment 4 times a year' at which point I whip out some coloured gels a length of copper wire and a flashlight and she waves me through

12/28 Revenge Fantasy #1647J6436d: Picture this Sean: It's 11:30 on a Monday morning in the midtown offices of Forveaux Forveaux Forveaux & Partners LLP - I've never been there but I know the layout like the back of my hand: it's a sprawling ultramodern suite of offices - big front reception area - Bauhaus chairs potted plants - off to the left a conference room with a big long oak table - modern art on off-white walls - cubicles with glowing computer screens - Manhattan skyline backdrop streaming in through big wall-length windows - Peter's office is right at the end of the hall: he's sitting behind his desk of polished walnut $800 specs balanced on the bridge of his nose thumbing through a new brief - Gore City Cattle Prods hereinafter 'The Plaintive' blah blah blah - deadly boring stuff as you know yourself Sean - it's not long before Pierre's attention starts to wander - in the back of his mind a little door swings open and suddenly it's 10 yrs ago and once again he's imposing his perverted will on my future girlfriend forcing her to suck his horrible disgusting penis - she's gagging and choking and hot tears of shame and revulsion are burning down her cheeks but his greasy Gallic will is implacable he holds her in place till the job is done - Pierre pushes back from the desk and looks down at his member its livid spongy head now sharply outlined against costly pants fabric - to hell with the client coming in at 12 thinks Le Frog the sating of my lust takes precedence and with that he unzips his fly fully bent on autogratification - just then Stephanie Hill walks in with papers for him to sign - Le Frog leaps up and starts chasing her around the room tongue snaking in and out all black and thick and shiny promising her furs and diamonds and holidays in Antigua in exchange for permission to introduce Mr. Dong to Little Miss Muffet - poor Stephanie's tripping on her heels frantic to get away and Peter's chasing her puffing and panting and hissing you're probably not as tight as my little girlfriend helas non but you're tight enough for jazz come to Pierre my proud beauty - meanwhile Agent Prendergast has just entered the building - I take the elevator up to the X Floor - I walk along the corridor following the arrows on the wall to Suite XXX - I'm well turned out so they buzz me right in - I have a tan raincoat draped casually over my arm very Dick Powell - I march straight past reception - Excuse me sir you can't - I march on down the hall reading the name plates on the doors - aha! Here we are - no knock just enter - not a moment too soon: Stephanie's backed into a corner hair all messed up trying to fend off the foul fiend with a desk lamp - when Forveaux sees me he tucks his shirt in and darts back behind his desk - Stephanie gives me a startled / grateful look of rek - I give her a reassuring smile and then with quiet authority: 'I take mine black with 6 sugars Ms. Hill' - she throws an anxious glance at Le Flog and hurries out - alone at last!! - Forveaux stares at me - he's leaning forward with one shaggy eyebrow raised: 'an' you har miztare—?' - in one fluid motion I whip

the raincoat aside and he's suddenly face to barrel with McSplatter
- the other eyebrow goes up - pale and frowning he leans back - This
is no time for fancy speeches 'because you this because you that' - I
bear my teeth in a tight dry grin: THIS IS FOR AMELIA GARRITY
YOU FRENCH FUCK and without further ado I plug him fast +
clean - D'UM! D'UM! D'UM! - one in the head 2 in the heart

Leyes de honor son más que divinas leyes

as the poet Calderon remarks - I don't wait around to inspect my
handiwork I turn on my heels and walk out of the room - outside in
the hall as you'd expect there's a good deal of hysterical screaming
and crying he shot Mr. Forveaux oh God oh God oh my God etc.
- glancing neither right nor left Prendy The Perp marches back
the way he came - of course the really classy thing would be to toss
my business card on the receptionist's desk or better still I could
get Stephanie to stick out her tongue for the host - 'card of Prendy'
- 'Amen' - poor Stephanie who's crouching in terror with a couple
of sister wage slaves beside the water cooler - but that would entail
getting new cards made as all I have are my old ones

Being as I'm armed and extremely dangerous marching through the halls with the murder weapon in plain view I probably *would* make it out of the building - I'm sure I'd have the elevator all to myself - the doorman ducks down under his desk as I stroll past - but outside it's a different story: wafting crisply to my ears on the chilly January (?) air I hear sirens - New York's Finest are on their way! - Prendy blows out his cheeks heaves a sigh and lights a Parliament - I might even sit down on the front steps to wait for them - calmly smoking watching the traffic and the people going by with McSplatter sleeping warm in my waistband - no on second thoughts I'd better be on my feet when the boys in blue arrive - in next to no time 4 cruisers and 2 cop vans appear lights flashing sirens wailing - they disgorge swat teams tear gas megaphones Waco lights the works - 2 cop copters float overhead - this is Kathy Jo Normal for Fox Channel 5 reporting live from the crime scene etc. - sorry Kathy Jo spoilsport that I am I'm going to sabotage your GUNMAN IN MIDTOWN SIEGE opener by tossing McSplatter with a clatter at the feet of a white-faced rookie - I take one last drag on my ciggy - I hold my paws out for the bracelets - click! - I'm led away - a power-suited media maven yells: tell us why you did it! - In response I begin to recite *On Raglan Road* by the late Patrick Kavanagh in a passable imitation of the master's flinty baritone but no friends of poesy they the brutish coppers toss me in the van and slam the doors and we're off at a clip to central booking

All right Sean let's pause for a mo and examine this little fantasy - you'll notice I *don't* get away with it - I don't even *try* to get away with it!! - now that's all well and good and very romantic and I'm sure Amelia would be flattered to know I was so into avenging her ghost that I didn't care tuppence what happened to me afterwards - on the other hand by the beard of St. Francis I HAVE TO GET AWAY WITH IT - not because I personally want to live - I really don't - but because

I have a sacred duty to MR. SEMTEX and GUMBY and YOUNG WITCH OF TRIM and the teeming hordes of other Prendian brain-children yet unborn - with me gone the way of lethal injection *who will give them life?* - There's nobody I can anoint / pass the chalice to: if there's one person who understands my vision it's Ken Privette but the sad truth is that Ken is TECHNICALLY INCOMPETENT - back in '91 I brought him in as A.D. on MAKE ME COME YOU WHITE BASTARD a straightforward 4 min. short but he nearly wrecked the whole project - so you see Sean *I have to get away with it* - I have to plan my getaway - if I don't get that sorted I'm going to end up sitting on Death Row with 25 mins to go waiting for them to jab me in the arm with enough tranks to kill a charging elephant

OPERATION SNUFFOUT - BASIC KIT:
1. McSplatter (+ silencer - remind me to buy one)
2. getaway car with A+ turbo acceleration / power steering / RADIO / CD PLAYER WITH FAT SPEAKERS (investigate car rental = Raptor's Visa Gold???)
3. some sort of disguise???

———·———

12/29 2 P.M. REVENGE FANTASY #3243534343T:
Scene: the Forveaux summer house on Cape Cod - Peter's lounging in a hammock in the den in his Bill Blass casuals a $300 cashmere sweater draped about his shoulders sipping his chardonnay watching hockey on the sports channel - Prendy the Fly on the Wall glares down at The Accused from the picture molding with my 800 eyes or however many eyes I have glares down in patient smoldering hatred wishing I was a mosquito loaded with an industrial strength dose of malaria ready willing and able to bury my stinger in the pulp of his hairy earlobe - Calmly rubbing my forelegs together I study my prey: his hair is too long at the back his eyebrows are bushy his sideburns

are gray - it's that revolting middle-aged swinger look - good God almighty Sean it suddenly dawns on me who he looks like - he looks like BURT BACHARACH - This is terrible - Bacharach is one of my idols - how dare Forveaux look like Lord Melody the King of Song! - But that's life isn't it - full of nasty surprises

———

12/29 3 P.M.: I'm happy to report I was totally wrong: The resemblance between Forveaux and Burt Bacharach = v. slight / practically nonexistent - Deeply troubled I dashed over to Tower Records - the one on B'way - up on the mezz. if you ferret around in Show Tunes you eventually hit their shamefully scrappy Bacharach selection - I was looking for the maestro's mug shot - There he was: Burt looking amazingly young with short back and sides grinning sheepishly in a tux w/ La Dietrich standing behind him - No use - too young . . . Dionne . . . More Dionne . . . Dionne and Dusty! I used to have that album (Memo to Rhino: rerelease me) . . . On . . . On . . . Still no pix of the mature maestro . . . Aha! This is more like it: the cover of *Another Fifth Rate Trib. To the Genius of Burt B by Bands You've Never Heard Of* has a nice up-to-the-minute shot of BB sitting at the johanna with one hand up in the air (what the world needs now etc.) - Drink him in lads and lassies: note the blistering rays of SOUL GENIUS beaming out of that noble profile - this is the face of a man of virtue a man of wit of grace not a loathsome lecher!!! - Forveaux's features are infinitely courser and more lupine - You have to remember I only saw him for 15 seconds and I was drunk off my tiddily - how did I ever get it into my head that he looked like Burt? - When Good Brain Cells Go Bad etc.- anyway much relieved I continued browsing in Show Tunes / Popular Vocalist Male / Popular Vocalist Female because a weirdly cute pierced youngster had suddenly appeared a few ft. to my right - picture Prendy pretending to read the back of a Rod Stewart CD while surreptitiously checking out the bootiful hottie: kohl black eyes psychotic-vacant expression bright cluster of nose rings / plastered down Josephine Baker hair - Fake (?) beauty spot / green leather hot pants / PINK gogo boots / seethru blue plastic Barbarella cape!!! - Behold ye happy gods who live forever a Child of Tomorrow is reading the liner notes to the Sinatra boxed set and no power in heaven or earth can stop her from buying it - if she doesn't have the readies by God I'll buy it for her - as I remember telling Amelia the hottie's spiritual sister once you've grasped the key points of Sinatra's Life you begin to see how the twisted minds behind the military industrial entertainment complex will stop at nothing to nurture and sustain human greed and depravity in preparation for the second coming of Queen Father in the Satanic Fathership a time beyond nightmare when the hideously reanimated corpses of JFK and Marilyn Deano Sammy Frankie Peter Lawford Bob Hope Princess Grace of Monaco and countless other dead Hollywood celebrities will be made to jerk and prance like hideous puppets to the obscene beat of the bongo drum - Rebel Rebel must have felt my mottled gaze burning into her nape because she suddenly swung around stuck a pierced tongue out at me and walked off - Why am I so attracted to Doomed Youth?

Dec. 30 / 1 A.M.: It just hit me Sean: looking in the Yellow Pages is bullshit - what I need is a Who's Who of NY NJ CT lawyers - And where might one score such a volume? From a lawyer of course but the only lawyer I know (apart from yourself and McGrath) is Ward Javitt the twit I hired to sue the Romanian who ripped me off over the Freytag Self-Tuning Drum Kit patents - at one point during my Affluent Years I had 3 and a half grand invested in an invention called the Freytag Self-Tuning Drum Kit - a mentally deranged Serb named Marko came up with the basic design - I showed you my old business cards - anyway it was a potential goldmine but we were double-crossed by a dirty little Romanian slime called Ionescu (you can't make this stuff up) - Ward swore we could nail him 'but good' but Ward was full of shit - I tore up Javitt's business card in a fit of pique one morning on the steps of the Brooklyn courthouse - he's not in the book - he was always a very shady character - by now he's probably disbarred and fled to S. America - There's only one thing for it: first thing tomorrow morning I hit the libraries

---

For starters it turns out there's no such thing as the New York Bar Association - it's the Association of the Bar of New York City - I spoke to a nice lady stationed at the library desk of said Assoc. and in my best imitation of Liam 'I'll Chorm the Panties Off Ya' Neeson I explained to her that I was trying to find an old school chum who I'd heard was practicing law in the Big Apple blah blah - Gosh you know I'd really like to find him Gosh you know - I was told to go to the Biz and Science Library at 34th and Madison and consult the *Martindale-Hubbell Law Directory* - Ta bye slam - Out the door like a bolt of lightning Vincent shouting after me: Stop! Where are you going? Come back! You're fired! - I sprinted across to the F - off at 34th - legged it across to Madison - up the steps of Biz and Science - big shiny metal doors (what's this - a maximum security library??) - I was directed downstairs - the guy at the desk a fat bearded guy he looked a little bit like Borges in his Fernando Rey phase huffed and puffed and eventually handed over the goods - *Martindale-Hubbell* Volume 12 / New York - a chunky tome! Come here to me my morocco-bound beauty let me suck on your paper paps - I retreated to the far end of the room - smooth PA girl's voice: 'the library will be closing in 5 minutes' - frantic thumbing thumbing thumbing - white pages . . . blue pages . . . white pages . . . of course they started turning off the lights - sir the library is closing - just a minute - sir the library - get off my toe man get off my toe - in the end there were 3 of them trying to pull the book away from me but I clung on for dear life and just as they were prying my fingers loose I startled them with a joyful shout

BREAKTHROUGH!!!!!!!
I FOUND HIM
I FOUND HIM
RING OUT YOU SOLSTICE BELLS
I FOUND THE BASTARD
J'AI TROUVE LE PRICK
LET THE GAMES BEGIN

————•————

COMMAND POST 12/30 - 11:15 P.M.: Oh oh oh the godlike power of knowledge Sean the head rush of discovery!! - Lytton Hershon Kaiser Forveaux Mendez LLC - let the Exterminating Angel take note - have their offices at 261 Fifth Ave - Suite 904 - the cross street is 29th - I burst out of Biz and Science and immediately hit the pay phone on the corner - I called The Number - with dry mouth and trembling hands I waited through all eternity for a receptionist to pick up and tell me where Froggy was having dinner tonight - but no one picked up they'd all left for the day 'please call back during normal business hrs' - the disappointment was good: it brought me down to earth - I started walking east lost in thought - I could smell it: this was going to be a long campaign - Patience and Pacing would be of the essence - Patience and Pacing and Perseverance and - not to be scoffed at - the Power of Prayer

O Great Artemis
Mistress of the Hunt
may this humble offering

of wine-soaked
origami mice
be pleasing to Thy sight
may Thy prattling pup Prendy
do what he has to do
and see it through without exemption
till Le Frog
is no more
amen

———•———

One of the nice things about living where you work is that you're always in before the boss har har wink wink ('Good *morning* Mr. Szabo!') - I can see my new up-with-the-larkness makes Old Grumpy Grouch white with rage - and him just back from a week sunning his buns down the Florida keys!! - I was going to give you a STALKER update but there isn't time - it's 8:45 and time to do my exit-to-come-back-in routine thereby avoiding Jeff A.K.A. Robbie the Robot the official opener-upper who has an annoying habit of showing up promptly at 9:30 if not before - I'm going to nip down the street to the Italian pastry shop hang out there for half an hr. read the paper stroll back up for a 9:32 entrance: 'Morning Jeff' - he glances up at the clock - can't believe the old time bandit has turned over a new leaf ha ha ha

———•———

New Year's Eve: Well Sean by rights I should be out there whooping it up with the rest of them celebrating The Big Breakthrough slash the end of another wonderful year on the prison planet - I had Privette on the blower half an hour ago trying to lure me out to Williamsburg to go with him to a bands-plus-hi8-shorts fest that awful woman Cindy is organising - normally I'd've gone just for the hell of it but this year

I'm proud to say I stood firm - this New Year's I've decided to stay home and work: I've got an important assassination to plan plus I want to bring the Dossier on the Accused up to date - I'd better get cracking because by 11 o'clock you know there'll be hordes of drunken bridge & tunnel clowns stumbling up and down Henrietta shrieking their heads off spontaneously disrobing vomiting in the gutter etc.- Depending on how much work I get done I may permit myself one small glass of Jägermeister at the stroke of midnight - we'll pause and drink a solemn toast to the future success of STALKER and SNUFFOUT - then I'll read a few pages of Baudelaire shove some cotton wool in my ears and hopefully fall asleep - no Sean this New Year's is different: this year we omit the frivolity

———

New Year's Day: terrifying hangover - Command Post is closed until further notice - New Year's resolution: ABSTAIN from the stag syrup - it's lethal stuff and should be banned - immediate task = score a six of Bud and some Valium

———

'Lytton Hershon Kaiser Forveaux Mendez. Good morning.'

'Goot mhorning. Pierre Forveaux pleez.'

'May I ask what this is in reference to?'

'Der Dreyfus Case.'

'Please hold I'll connect you with Mr. Forveaux's secretary.' (click)

'Good morning. Mr. Forveaux's line.'

'Stephanie?'

'No this is Paula.'

'Vere iss Stephanie?'

'I'm afraid Stephanie isn't with us any more.'

'Aha! Anuzer wictim of his fuck unt fire policy.'

'Excuse me? Who is this—?'

Click - disengage probe - grinning Agent P. hangs up and saunters back to Kwik whistling the theme from *The Magnificent 7* - First Contact Sean First Contact

————

Janurary 3rd 7:20 A.M.: Insight of the Day: I NEED TO BUY A SUIT - Why should be obvious: I'm in no position to pay someone to put a tail on Pierre - Hiring pros like Burke and Max the Silent would be nice but the reality is I'm going to have to do it all myself - and for that I need a suit - Most of the places a top NY lawyer frequents in the course of a busy shystering day are places they won't let you in without a suit: posh restaurants judge's chambers etc. - I have to be able to pass through the tall gates of the citadel and stroll the corridors of power unmolested - a curt nod to the security robot at the front desk and I'm waved through - then it's Prendy P.I. on the job never letting Le Frog out of my sight for a nanosecond as he strides away across the courthouse atrium his one-of-a-kind handmade Italian leather soles echoing on the white marble tiles - I used to have a suit - as a matter of fact back in '88 at the height of Prendian Affluence I had 4 or 5 - but times got tough Sean I had to swallow my pride and pawn 'em - I wouldn't be surprised if some drug dealer got shot in my double breasted - it was a real How You Like Me Now I'm Your Pimp Baby sort of suit - lime green big wide lapels 3 buttons big breast pocket - Martha bullied me into buying it for our wedding - given a choice I'd have worn my leather jacket and my docs but I was outvoted as usual - yes I got married in that suit - and later at the party Uncle Fernando the thumping great fairy threw up all over me in the jakes - but that's another story (as the Handpeople say)

Jan 4: Efforts to score a suit should be in full swing but instead I'm forced to deal with incredibly aggravating peripheral bullshit: a crisis has developed re storing my stuff at Ken's - apparently Maude snapped no doubt in response to the pull of the moon and threw everything out on the street - Ken called 5 minutes ago to tell me the dam had burst - he managed to wangle a 24 hr. stay of execution from milady - oh thank you gracious Elvira let me kiss your glossy black toenails - so I have to find somewhere to stash my stuff multo pronto - there's no room at Kwik - LIFE Sean it's one fucking thing after another

Jan 5 - 4:10 A.M.: what we're seeing here is Hate - Hate humming away fully operational in its purest form - Maude dislikes me she distrusts me she's always resented my friendship with her husband - Result: she couldn't do it - she couldn't hold off for one more day - Privette calls me up here at 2 this morning - Hey listen she threw your stuff out - Again?? She threw my stuff out *again??* Why didn't you stop her? - Hey look I tried you know - what price friendship Sean I ask you - upshot I had to get a cab over to E. 5th at 2:30 in the morning and rescue my belongings off the sidewalk - Listen Ken I'm totally fucked now you do realise that - Jarleth calm down - No it's true I can't possibly hide all this shit at Kwik. Face facts Ken this time your woman has totally screwed me - in the end hee hee I guilt tripped him into springing for a 2 weeks rental at a storage hole on 2nd and 2nd - I got him to pay for the cab over as well - No Remorse: I've far too much on my plate - I have a man to murder - I can't be worrying about my gear getting kicked up and down the street!! - give me a break

———•———

Jan 5: 8 A.M.: Let's review: 1. The Bacharach Crisis is behind me 2. my gear's safely stashed - NO MORE DISTRACTIONS - pedal to the metal and on to VICTORY!!! SUIT ACQUISITION IS KEY

———•———

Jan. 5 Noon: It's a hard fact of life Sean but one I have to groove with: in pursuit of the Greater Good it sometimes happens that we have to put our pride our amour propre on hold and bow down before the Altar of Imbecilica Dominatrix Mundi A.K.A. Mistress Silly Billy Queen of All There Is - Fact: I need a suit - Fact: I don't have $$$ to buy a suit - Raptor on the other hand is on excellent terms with all the major credit card companies - they even send her Xmas cards!!! - ergo after hours of internal struggle I'm forced to the conclusion that Raptor and Prendy must be Reconciled - yes it's a chilling thought and I balk at it - mentally I'm rearing eyes rolling neighing in terror but I don't see any other way - I have to remember it'll only be temporary: a temporary misalliance - So I took a deep breath did a Jägermeister shot and called her

———•———

Several hrs later there we were in the suit dept. of Tomorrow's Guy on 5th Ave: me standing in front of a full length mirror quivering from head to toe with boredom and irritation Raptor standing behind me beaming at my reflection with her head cocked to one side Lawrence the salesman surreptitiously glancing at his watch trying to stifle a yawn - and why shouldn't he yawn? Hadn't she kept us prisoners here for over 2 hrs??? - I'd been forced in and out of that dressing room 5000000 times in and out in and out try this on try that on try on the other one again

'Jarleth - try on the blue one again'

'But I don't *like* the blue one Gwyneth'

'Try on the green one then'

'No!'

'Jarleth—'

'NO! NO! NO! NO! N.O. MEANS NO!'

and with that Prendergast turned to the startled Lawrence: The circus is over my good man. I'm taking the grey one - I turned and marched towards the checkout - Raptor followed - she rummaged around for a year and a day in her purse and at long last up popped the Visa Gold - the checkout girl handed over the goods: thank you sir for shopping at Tomorrow's Guy - thank YOU for having such a hot young bod my gorgeous pantera - and clutching our shopping bags we exited the cloth emporium - Prendy's Stalking Kit: suit 1 winter weight grey - shirts white x 2 - ties silk x 3 - socks wool x 3 pair - shoes Italian-made 1 pair black - I tried to get Raptor to spring for a nice cashmere coat and a summer suit as well but she wouldn't do it - still and all it's not a bad haul: as of today Prendy is fully kitted out for Uptown Stalking 'n' Ting - Of course no sooner were we out on the street than Raptor sprang into chirpy organisational mode - she started mapping out the rest of the First Day of Our New Life Together - only a short cab ride away she said there was a cozy little Italian place where the linguini was to die for and the waiters sang sweet old Italian folk songs and Broadway show tunes - out of the corner of my eye I spied a cab turning onto 5th - Jarleth we must celebrate! - Gwyneth? - yes? - Goodbye - I yanked the third bag (ties socks shoes) from my astonished future partner in life and dived out into the traffic - TAXI!!! - the cab screeched to a halt and I leapt in with my purchases - she was right behind me screaming raining kicks and blows on my faithless rump - I slammed the door and off we sped - Goodbye Esmerelda Prendy's Bane goodbye goodbye - you're better off without me Gwyneth - cue Ann Murray singing 'Snowbird' - endless bird you cannot change - hi ho silver away

- That lady is your wife

No question mark - a matter-of-fact statement from my driver a Sikh gentleman bearded and burly - 2 dark eyes twinkling at me in the rearview mirror

- Yes Mr. Singh my heart's delight she was my wife but now I'm free- free as a bloody bird so it's down and across at a smart clip please to Loisida - On a coaster on a bartop in a bar on the NW corner of 13th and B stands a tall majestic pint of jet black foamtopped goodness with my name on it!

- 13th and B. Very good sir

I love New York!

Monday Jan 6 6:15 A.M.: Now I've got my boss threads the next step is to quit Kwik and dedicate myself body and soul to stalking - hang on a minute says Sean what are you going to live on? - that's a very good point I'm glad someone's paying attention - another thing I have to take into account is the Future of the Command Post - it's hard enough keeping it going as it is - as you know I live in perpet. fear of discovery (recurring dream: I'm fast asleep on the couch in Vincent's office all snug and warm - I open my eyes and there's Vincent bending over me his Nixonesque jowls wobbling with rage - I try to explain that I suddenly felt ill and had to lie down but he's already screaming for the gendarmes and whacking me with his cane) - If I quit Kwik it's tantamount to kissing the Post goodbye and that's obviously not on - much as I'd love to give Vincent the finger and turn my back on the Zombie House forever I can't - not yet - instead I have to be super-pragmatic and continue to strive ever upwards like Goethe's Faust: the challenge is to find a way to stalk AND earn my daily crust - Tomorrow is Tuesday = my day off = Stalking Kicks Off - Wednesday I call in sick - I stay out for at least a week or as long as I can get away with and in the meantime I stalk Froggy DAY AND NIGHT - after that I'll continue stalking on my days off - if I'm still at it 3 months down the road so be it - whatever it takes to get the job done and nail Pierre to the wall - so for now it's GOODBYE DAYS OFF!!! Goodbye happy carefree afternoons blockbuster-hopping at the Loew's up on 79th St. - goodbye liquid lunches at Firewaters & nights on the town with Privette getting bollocksed - when duty calls Prendy stands up straight and tall out of homicidal dreams and puts on his hunting finery

---

PROJECT STALKER / DAY ONE: TUES. 7th JAN

The yellow fingers of New York winter dawn creeping over Vincent's smelly shag carpet proclaim that the fateful day is here: the Royal

Hunt of the Frog is about to begin - Master of Hounds - yes m'lud - distribute the goblets of steaming port! - the dogs are restless m'lud - Of course they are! Down Growler! Lurcher to heel! Fret not my barking boys we'll soon be flying across the concrete meadows with the scent of rank Fo(rveau)x in our nostrils quickening our canine hearts coating our happy yowling tongues with pink saliva - but first the brushing of the teeth the ritual once over wetting crown to sole with a damp cloth A.K.A. Prendy's Morning Ablutions - after donning fresh boxers undershirt warm wool socks it's buzz buzz shave the morning bristles - next I repair to my Secret Wardrobe in the back storeroom - here I select a crispy snow-white shirt and a red and blue silk tie - hand-stitched just for me by smiling Asian child workers - I throw open the other locker to reveal (drum roll) My Stalking Suit - The Grey - I put it on - next I slip into my new ultra comfy black Italian all-leather uppers - aside from a shower and a hot tub the one important amenity the Command Post sorely lacks is a full-length mirror but by standing on a crate in the men's I'm able to check myself out knee to neck - very nice - dapper and distinguished - next Prendy P.I. puts on his shades - my black frame Raybans which I haven't worn since Cum Jerk days - I grab my trench coat and my copy of Saturday's *Times* - wait a minute - my God I almost forgot something muy importante: my opera glasses!!!! - I found these little beauts quite by chance in a junk shop last Friday - one look Sean and I knew they were an essential part of the kit - I made the earhooks out of coat hangers and soldered (or as they say over here soddered) them on - I put them in my pocket and set forth: up with the grill - I step out on to the street - it's a nasty morning - chilly windy wet - I'm going to grab a cup o' joe at the little diner on the corner of Henrietta and Sullivan - I'll be off in a minute to get the F at W. 3rd - It's now 7:22 - plenty of time - whoever heard of a lawyer getting to the office before 9:30!!!?

DAY ONE: STALKER'S REPORT

Exhausting day Sean - v. frustrating too - I got up to 29th and 5th c. quarter to 8 and immediately took up position at the bus stop across the street from 261 Fifth Ave - there are obvious drawbacks to watching a building from a bus stop but stalkers can't be choosers - NYC bus shelters have glass on only 2 sides and an icy wet wind was whipping down the avenue - I turned up the collar of my coat and unfolded my pretreated copy of the *Times* and held it up in front of me - the wind was battering away at it but to thwart the elements I'd reinforced the pages with Scotch tape - my head & upper torso were completely hidden - working one-handed I removed my shades and fished my opera glasses out of my coat pocket and slipped them on - the idea is to keep both hands free to hold up the *Times* so I look like Mr. Typical Working Stiff waiting for the bus engrossed in his morning paper - in reality Sean I was staring out through the 2 little spyholes I'd drilled in the A section: my telescopic gaze was trained on the glass lobby doors of 261 - I was amazed how well they worked! - I could see the expression on the doorman's face - he was talking on the phone writing in his notepad sipping his coffee nodding and saying good morning to the incomers - I could nearly read his lips - 15 min. went by - mentally I was screaming come on Forveaux don't let me down - Make the scene you bastard make my day - by the powers vested in me by hate and animal magnetism I command you to appear - I was afraid I wouldn't recognise him that I'd catch a 2 second glimpse of the back of his head and I wouldn't be sure if it was him or not - You'll know him I kept telling myself you'll know him - And then suddenly THERE HE WAS standing by the front desk holding a cup of coffee - Mr. Euro Patrician hatless in a stylish tan overcoat w/ a fur collar - it was Peter Sean Peter-Pierre in the flesh honouring me with his coarse lupine profile as he

paused for a spot of pseudoegalitarian banter with the doorman - I
clocked him for a full 10 seconds before he turned away and disappeared walking towards the elevators - my heart was hammering
my hands were shaking - 2 seconds later a bus pulled up totally
blocking my view - I could so easily have missed him! - After The
Sighting the inevitable anticlimax - Now what? - He's inside - I'm
out here in the cold - my coffee buzz was starting to wear off - what
was I going to do? Hang around out here w/ my opera glasses glued
to the entrance patiently counting the hours hoping and praying he
comes out??? What if he didn't come out? - what if he stayed inside
all fucking day? It was quite conceivable I wouldn't be vouchsafed
another glimpse of him until 6 o'clock - A workaholic mightn't show
until 9 or 10!!!! - I knit my brows - I was dying for a fag but I couldn't
pander to the craving because I had to keep holding the shagging
paper up - my arms were getting tired - I'd just decided to retire
somewhere warm to rethink my strategy when one of the glass
doors of 261 opened and Forveaux came out - he turned left - my
right - and started walking towards 28th - I lost him for a second
when a van went by - there he was: standing at the corner - he was
hailing a cab! - I whipped off my opera glasses and dropped the
paper - waving my arm I stepped into the street - a cab pulled up
- I dived in

'Quick follow that cab!'

'Which one sir? I see 4 . . .'

'Jesus Christ he's getting away you fucking eejit! After him! After
him!'

'I will not be called names in my own cab sir'

'I'm sorry—'

'Please get out sir'

'I said I was sorry. Here's 20 bucks—'

'No no. Get out please.'

'Look here my friend I'm an Irishman. Mindful of the centuries of suffering inflicted upon both our peoples by British imperialism—'

'No sir. I have a tire iron in my glove compartment. I will hit you over the head with it. I am not joking. Get out please.'

I got out - Touchy Turban zoomed off - I walked down 5th - I went into a diner and sat up at the counter - I ordered a coffee and a jelly donut and stared at defenseless eggs being slowly murdered on the hot plate - after a couple of minutes I pulled myself together and went back out into the cold - I bought another *Times* and gouged fresh spyholes in it with my Swiss army knife - I walked back to the bus stop - I sat down on the low wall behind the stop and smoked a cig all the time keeping my eyes peeled for cabs pulling up across the street - it was only 9:15 - yes it was going to be a long campaign - long campaign is right: the fucker didn't show again until nearly 6 o'clock - he got out of his cab and practically ran inside - 20 min. later he came out again - he hopped in another cab - I did the same - this time my driver was a sunny laughing man from the islands and only too delighted to land a bit part in a Hitchcock thriller - I sat beside him hawkeyed in the thickening winter dusk - Where is he? You fucking lost him didn't you? - No no man relax relax everything's A-OK trust me ha! ha! ha! - Delacroix was an excellent driver - he kept right behind le Frog without being obtrusive - I was willing Froggy to stop at a bar or a restaurant or better still some seedy sinister doorman building in the West 80s - Apt XX: home of Madame du Paine high-class dominatrix - instead the subject made a beeline for Grand Central Station where I watched him board the 6:49 to Birchmont - sitting in that window seat with his specs on reading *Newsweek* he looked just like any other tired middle-aged businessman going home to the missus after a long hard day screwing the gen. pub. - that was it Sean: Day One

Yes Sean I see you - jumping up and down on your little cloud with your halo in your hand pointing at the big screen behind you - all right let's take a look - what's playing tonight at the Celestial Cinaplex?- Why it's *Married to the Mob* - yes as a matter of fact I *do* remember the opening scene of *MTTM* where Pfeiffer's husband (one of the Baldwins?) quietly plugs the guy through the back of the seat on the train - sorry to disappoint you but I already thought of that and it won't work re Le Frog for the following reasons: (1) I'd need an accomplice - someone to sit beside me and cover me with his *Financial Times* while I screw on the silencer and do the plugging and (2) I don't want an accomplice (3) more importantly it's difficult (I don't say impossible) to shoot someone through the back of a Metro North seat because those seats happen to have thick metal strips running vertically over the wood frames - wait a minute how on earth could I possibly know that? - aha! - if you spend enough time hanging out in bars Sean you eventually acquire all the wisdom of the ages

STALKER: DAY 2 - WEDNESDAY 6:58 A.M.

Horrible night - tossing and turning - nightmares - at one point I dreamt I was directing a Stevie Wonder video - we were shooting in a maximum security prison-cum-public library - Stevie was singing his new hit 'Part Time Stalker' which was 'Part Time Lover' except the lyrics were about what a fucking eejit I am and how Forveaux knows I'm stalking him and he's secretly laughing at me - 'he's laughin' at you Pren-der-gast / you really are a stupid ass . . .' etc. - it was extremely unpleasant - Martha was in it - she turned up as head warden of the women's section - at one point I was down on my knees in front of the whole crew begging her to let us shoot a scene in the women's showers but she wouldn't hear of it - she stood with her hands on her hips in camo fatigues black army boots glinting shaking her shaved head - she looked like Sigourney Weaver in *Alien 3* - in the end 2 of her amazonian lieutenants dragged me off to solitary for a good flogging - at which point I woke up in protest against all the symbolism - So here we are: DAY 2 - 15 mins ago I nipped out to the pay phone on the corner and called in sick - putting on my sickliest wheeziest voice I told Vincent I was down w/ the flu - presently I'm about to exit the Command Post - my 6th sense tells me this is it: today's the day we're going to SHAKE SOME ACTION

STALKER DAY 3

Same as Day 2 = Nothing - my driver - a surly Pole - refused the commission - 'No! I don't follow nobody' and pulled over to the curb - I leaned forward and gave him a sharp clip on the ear and jumped out - this being New York there was another cab 2 ft. away - I dived in - a tiny little woman pressed into the backseat started screaming her head off - the driver swung round - I immediately recognised former Soviet foreign minister Molotov - apologizing I backed out and slammed the door - I turned around - the Pole grabbed my shirt front and kneed me in the groin - I walked to the curb and lay down - it was all downhill from there

STALKER DAY 4

Nothing - My hopes were raised only to be dashed by a brief pitstop at a florist in the East 30s - I was excited beyond words to see Forveaux return to his cab with a big bunch of daffs - I had a flash of him presenting them to a foxy-psychotic Bronx Science 11th grade Amelia lookalike A.K.A. his coy mistress but no: on we drove to Grand Central where he caught the choo-choo to Birchmont as usual - Madame Forveaux: 'Flowers! Oh Pierre are these for me?' - 'Who else ma chérie? (unsuspecting flabby clown-spouse!!)'

Le weekend: he's up in Westchester doing God knows what - I'm stuck down here in the city bereft of wheels - I feel totally impotent - Oh to have a zippy little rental car and be able to tail him on family outings to Bear Mt. and the Berkshires!!! - What was I thinking?? I should have stuck like glue to Raptor the Faery of The Money Tree!!!!! - But I couldn't do it Sean: when she smiles like that - like Glinda the Good Witch in the *Wizard of Oz* serenading the Munchkins - come out come out wherever you are - I want to throttle her I want to reign down blow after blow on her smug vegetable head whack whack whack with a lead pipe - no there's absolutely no doubt in my mind: running out on Gwyneth like that was the only honourable thing to do - otherwise I'd have ended up killing the wrong person

Sunday evening: There it was Sean parked under a streetlight on 16th St off 3rd: a lovely olive green vintage Volvo ES 1800 - it's the stationwagon version of The Saint's car - they only made about 400 of them - it's the ideal tailing / pursuit / getaway car - an ultra cool

'60s job low to the ground with that cool slanting back window - in tip-top condition too except for a hint of rust on the front right fender - *Alphaville Blow Up Point Blank Bullit:* I immediately saw myself behind the wheel zipping in and out of holes in the traffic with Forveaux just up ahead - it suddenly occurs to me it would be a brilliant car to die in the back of - listen to me Lemmy - Caution keeps his eyes fixed on the twisting turning midnight mountain road - Lemmy I'm not (cough) going to make it - sure you are kid. Hold on. We're only half an hour from the border - No really Lemmy look at me I'm bleeding to death I'm not going to make it - suit yourself kid and he shoots blind into the backseat with his police .38 - I gasp I grunt I flop around a bit I lie still

———•———

Day 5: nothing nada zilch - if I didn't hate him already I'd have grown to hate him because he's such a boring unadventurous bastard - he never does anything he never goes anywhere - the man has no social life - what the fuck is going on??? Ans: I'm blowing all my $$$$ on cabs and Scotch tape

———•———

Day 6: Nothing - subject bought copy of *Harper's* and boarded Birchmont train

———•———

1/16: There's a crisis Sean: Vincent left a terse message at Ken's (where the old fool thinks I live!) saying if I don't report for work tomorrow I'm fired - he says he knows I'm not really sick - I think I know what happened: one of the zombies must have spotted me uptown and ratted - it's par for the course Sean: Zombie House = Stool Pigeon Central - Re Pierre: Nada - nothing to report - stalkee boarded Birchmont train

———•———

Friday: I'm back at Kwik - Szabo's put me on the late shift for the whole week so I'm totally screwed - God give me strength - this is torture I should be out there stalking - otherwise what's the point?? - fucking Vincent's watching me like a hawk - I heard him yelling at Meshell this morning going on and on about a bad smell in his office (memo: air room upon rising) - Inner Voice: 'Forget stalking. Just stroll into Courtroom No.2 both barrels blazing and take him out' - Superego (sternly): 'No! You MUST get away with it' etc. - why must I? - everything seems so fucked up and pointless - it's the little things Sean the little things that get you down - for example on the floor at my feet beside the counter is a box of UPS envelopes - on the side of the box it says FORM # 010195201 MALE GYMNAST - so far so good - but if you look at a sample envelope it's a picture of a javelin thrower - A JAVELIN THROWER IS NOT A GYMNAST - throwing the javelin is track and field - can it be that I'm the only person in a country of 300 million to have noticed this? More to the point can it be I'm the only one who CARES? Clearly everyone else has taken a secret telepathic oath to pretend these shameful abuses of the language don't matter - 'Heck Mabel golly gee what's all the fuss about?' - so be it - it's a burden I'll shoulder alone - and once more I'm staring up at the strip lights - will night never come?

1/19: I tried to retrieve some of my odds and ends from the storage hole - a snotty know-it-all NYU type with shaved head and goatee told me I had to pay for the next week in advance or he couldn't let me in - that's the storage hole racket for you: they're oh so nice and accommodating in the beginning but as soon as they get your stuff on the other side of the wire mesh they turn vicious - I rang Privette at work and tried to get him to spring for another week but he wouldn't - apparently Maude's on the warpath - he let it slip that he'd paid for the first 2 weeks and she promptly had a fit - P.S. message from Maude: tell Jarleth any future messages for him on our machine will be erased - Bitch

Command Post / Mon. Jan 20 / 6.30 A.M.

Well Sean here goes nothing: today's my day off this week - Vincent can't touch me - According to Blake DEATH was begot by Satan upon his daughter Sin - Baudelaire says HOPE was begot upon Dame Death by her lover Satan - Emily D. says HOPE is a thing with feathers - put it all together and what have you got? - an oven stuffer with glowing red eyes - not very appetizing but I'll have a bite anyway - yes Sean you heard it here first I'm going to give it one more try: Let the talking drums speak to elephant and crocodile to antelope and wilderbeest and snake - let the news spread up and down the river: PRENDY COME - PRENDY STALK AGAIN

1/ 20: Nothing - stalkee boarded Birchmont train

Tues. 1/21: blasted out of Kwik at 5 on the dot to cover Pierre's evening exit - Report to follow

Sean

I jump back

I kiss myself

I kiss the air

I kiss the ground

I kiss the flag snapping in the breeze outside the Chelsea post office

I do a JB pants-ripping knee dive to the concrete screaming FRED can I hear the funky drummer Maceo Oh Maceo give it to the funky drummer FRED come on Robert come on fellahs make it FUNKY and the crowd's on their feet stomping and whistling as Fred Wesley and my manager and the tour doctor drape the American flag about my steaming shoulders and I'm dragged off stage kicking and screaming I feel good

The sun is shining - why oh why? - I'll tell you why: I've made a marvelous discovery Sean a truly marvelous discovery - sister come quick I've discovered Uranus - oh what have you found? says Sean what have you found? - All in good time my spirit guide all in good time - all will be revealed - suffice it to say this is the STALKING BREAKTHROUGH we've prayed for - may the Norns be praised! - if I'm not mistaken Sean they've just handed us Peter's bloody head on a silver platter

Ladies Divine!
Accept our humble thanks
Reynolds & Prendergast
Prostrate in the dust
Beg leave to kiss
Your proud pagan bosoms

———•———

Breakthrough Tues. 21st Jan: HOW IT HAPPENED

A couple of mornings ago Sean you let me blather on about Hope etc. but deep down we both knew it was the end of the line didn't we? -

Stalking was a Total Failure - when I arrived up at 261 Fifth Ave. yesterday evening after work I was only going through the motions - I was feeling totally wrecked - I'd had another night of fitful sleep Queen Mab shrieking and jumping up and down on my chest etc. followed by an endless boring day at Kwik - even armed with a flask of scalding black coffee I could barely keep my eyes open - 7 o'clock came and went - no action nothing not a glimpse not a sign - at last c. 7:35 P.M. Peter appeared - it had just started drizzling - he turned right and started walking towards 29th - Sean I was so out of it so tired and utterly demoralised that the right turn didn't register - at the corner of 29th he hailed a cab - I dragged myself to my corner and did the same - my driver was a wizened little chap with tinted glasses and stubbly cheeks - he looked a bit of a grumbler but he accepted my 20 without demur and the chase began - oh but his cab was nice and warm - I had to will myself to sit up straight and not fall asleep - outside the rain was starting to come down - my driver's ID photo caught my eye - now there's an inscrutable smile I thought - Hoque Malibar I murmured Hoque Malibar stay on his tail - it really was toasty warm in the backseat - my window was starting to steam up - I'd just started nodding off when suddenly the truth slapped me hard across the face - I came wide awake with a little shout: Going West! - He was going West Sean - West = AWAY from Grand Central!!!!!! - 29th runs west and Grand Central Station is EAST!!! - I rolled down my window and stuck my head out - it was true: we were turning onto 6th Ave. - a timorous tiny spark of HOPE ignited in my chest: could it be that at last something was happening?? - off 6th we hung a louie onto W. 34th - Hoque Malibar my friend listen you have to stay with him whatever you do we musn't lose him. Here - I flashed another Jackson - a thin dark paw reached back and snatched it - Hoque said nothing but I felt his concentration go up a notch - I could taste it Sean something *was* happening:

- oh where are you taking us? I asked the red tail lights visible 10 yds ahead - Quo vadis Satanus? - west west west the tail lights hissed - we turned on to 8th Ave. shabby sleazy old 8th Ave. and up we climbed with the rain falling harder now . . . into the 40s . . . Port Authority on our left . . . up up . . . into the strip bars zone: maybe he's going to a strip bar??? - We passed the Playpen where Amelia used to lap dance . . . yes my dear as you see I'm on the case . . . up up into the 50s . . . Columbus Circle . . . Into the 60s . . . on B'way now . . . Lincoln Plaza Cinema on the right where I took her to see *The Garden of The Finzi-Continis* on her 23rd (?) birthday . . . RED ALERT RED ALERT: Peter was turning left - Hoque Malibar followed him into a wedge of cabs: what's this? - A hotel - the Empire - a tryst in the penthouse suite?? - No - they continued to the corner - Peter got out and slammed the cab door - I got out too - I gave him a 5 second start: he crossed the street - and suddenly there she stood Sean rising up all majestic and floodlit in the dark and the rain all grand and twinkly-mysterious: LINCOLN CENTER A.K.A. Gotham's Premier Palace of Culture - Forveaux started up the steps - keep the grey-haired man in sight keep the grey-haired man in sight nothing else matters: he was 10 paces ahead of me walking across the front square or plaza with his grey head bent into the wind - Intense speculation: Why is he here? What's he going to see? What do they have here? - Theatre - Opera - Dance - where's the dance? - maybe he's going to the performing arts library? - how ironic! - In a previous life as a man of the theatre I used to come up here to do research: What do you mean you don't have Grotowski's love letters to his high school principal? This is an outrage etc. - keep the grey-haired man in sight - now he was cutting diagonally across the front sq. passing the famous fountain where Gene and Zero frolicked once upon a dream - I knew it I knew it!!! - he was making a beeline for the building with the tall windows the building with the big chandelier and the tall Chagalls = THE

MET - yes Sean: Pierre was going to THE OPERA!!! - As I pushed through the revolving doors I was cursing myself for leaving McSplatter back at the Command Post though of course yeah yeah we all know Rule No. 127564B: 'Never tail a stalkee into uncharted terr. if you're packing' - a good rule a sensible rule because yes we DO want to get away with it but on the other hand my God what a glorious place for an execution!! - I stepped into the lobby: and suddenly there they were the culturati all milling around: middle-aged lard arse matrons leading fish-faced husbands - well-heeled dudes with blinking neon signs strapped to their heads I'M A NEUROSURGEON I MAKE TOO MUCH MONEY - straggling groups of bullied brainwashed teens looking forlorn pale bored - you should be at home seducing the upstairs maid young lady - RED ALERT: a pair of hefty types in black paramil. sweaters w/ walkie talkies = Met Security - Note: they don't appear to be packing - mais où est le grey-haired man? - after several seconds of cold panic I locked onto him over by the 1st ticket window but Sean he wasn't alone there were people with him - the villain had erected a human shield!!! - I started walking towards the little group - they were having an orgy of 2 cheek kissy kissy - I clocked a woman c. Peter's age (the Clown-Spouse!??) a male about 19 (a nephew? a son??) and a teeny tiny little old woman - no not the Bergmanian horror from the Birchmont party this one had eyebrows (an aunt? a granny?) - I strolled right past them pretending I was looking for someone glancing at my watch etc. but really I was drinking them in especially the Clown-Spouse: she was tall and rail thin in a dark blue dress - gaunt face deep-set brown eyes - my God I thought is this woman really Amelia's mother?? - I saw no resemblance except that like mother like daughter she didn't look well - it's because you neglect me Pierre you neglect me terribly chasing after your schoolgirls. I shall put arsenic in your chocolat I shall I shall - the boy was tall too with short brown hair specs and the pimply visage of a seasoned masturbator - and yes the old lady was obviously the granny - she was frail and tiny with white hair watery blue eyes liver spots on her hands crab-apple cheeks - Pierre's face was still flushed from the cold - in his cashmere coat / red cravat he looked like a degenerate Caesar - as I walked past them he must have just said something funny because the Clown-Spouse was laughing and touching his arm - all at once booming in my head I heard a Greek Chorus: DO IT NOW DO IT NOW what are you waiting for this is your big chance he who hesitates is lost - who knows if you'll ever get this close to him again! - hang on though what about the security guys? - Meatheads doped up on steroids! They're half asleep! Nothing ever happens here! - but I don't have my gun - well go and get it - go and get it? - yes if you hurry you can get back for the intermission and plug him while he's standing on line for his wine spritzer - and what about the getaway? - fuck the getaway DO IT NOW DO IT NOW - while I was mentally wrestling with the Greeks believe it or not Sean a bald midget in a black Dracula cape appeared - he was walking through the crowd hitting a mini xylophone with a mallet to announce that it was Showtime - Peter started shepherding la famille round the corner - I followed them - on the other side of a fat pillar punters were queuing up - there were 3 or 4 guys some in Drac capes some in blazers all taking tickets - 'Ladies and gentlemen please step in if you're holding tickets. We're about to begin . . .' - there and then I decided to fetch McSplatter - I turned around and headed for the exit - out through the revolving doors into the cold wind and the rain - a scalper in an anorak tried to sell me orchestra seats - I shoved him aside and then I was running Sean full tilt across the square panting past the fountain - I hailed a cab - Henrietta St. driver and step on it - we got off to a fast start cruising down Columbus but in the 20s we hit one of those nighttime MEN AT WORK obstructions - wasted 10 precious minutes crawling past diggers jack hammers hardhats with red flags all lit up in that painful sodium glare - Upshot: we didn't make Henrietta St. till nearly half past 8 - I jumped out - so did the cabbie who was annoyed because I hadn't tipped him - actually I hadn't paid him at all because I'd blown all my cash on Hoque Malibar - Mr. Cabbie chased me down the street and very nearly caught me but I pulled out an extra burst of speed and he faded - I pulled away and left him shaking his fist and yelling after me - better safe than sorry I kept running for another 2 blocks then jogged around the corner and walked back up on Mulberry - red hot pains in my chest but still at liberty - no time to lose - down Henrietta - here's Kwik - out with keys - but the grill wasn't locked - it was down but it wasn't locked - I immediately smelt DANGER: Tuesday is our early night we close at 7:00 - so at 25 to 9 the grill should have been down AND locked - I got a flash of burglars working on the night safe cleaning us out - tomorrow there'd be cops swarming all over the shop and in the course of investigations they'd discover the Command Post - Greek Chorus: shoot him tonight nothing else matters focus on the mission get your gun - those Theban elders know best I thought: if there *are* thieves on the premises I'll just have to work around them - I opened the door and went in - it was pitch dark except for the EXIT sign glowing green on the far back wall - not a sound - I advanced super-quietly - and froze: there were 2 huge white eyes staring at me - it was only the giant plastic owl that sits on top of Alice Worth's computer - nearly gave me a heart attack - I continued towards the back - Wait! Sounds! Faint . . . muffled . . . I tiptoed forward - Sounds . . . coming from my bedroom!! - I crept up to the door and cupped my ear to the wood: from inside I heard gasps I heard groans and sighs - it took me a second to realise I was listening to the music of America and the World's No.1 indoor sport The Humpty Hump - in other words someone was having it off in Vincent's office - the Norns had struck again!! - how so? - because McSplatter was taped with duct tape to the bottom of Vincent's couch Sean and the rutting pair was probably getting busy *on* the couch - what to do? - Open the door flick on the light oh gosh God sorry you 2 I forgot something I won't be a sec please go about your business? - Nude / semi nude Pam and Jesus - it was probably Pam and Jesus - stare amazed as Prendy kneels before them to retrieve his piece - I straighten up tuck the gun in my waistband and wink: Mum's the word eh chums? - then I flick off the light and exit - of course with my luck Jesus would grab his brass knuckles or his stun gun and come after me - I turn he fires I wake up days later in Bellevue with badly burnt genitalia and no memory of the mission - contra caution the Greeks were chanting DO IT DO IT DO IT DO IT - hold on Greeks I can't let witnesses see me with McSplatter - DO IT DO IT DO IT DO IT DO IT - I gripped the door handle and pushed - it was locked - Just as well because a few seconds later the earth began to move: there were yelps and cries oh God oh God yes oh my God yes yes then a loud yelp followed by a distinctly female aaaaaaaaaaaah that melded with a manly huuuuuhhh - I realised they'd be up and about in no time looking for food and water - Hide! hissed the Greeks hide under Alice's desk then when the lovers leave you can slip out and get your gun. You'll still be in time to get back to the Met before the last curtain call - it seemed a good plan so I tiptoed over to Alice's desk and crawled in under - I waited 5 minutes - I waited 10 - Nothing stirring - they must have fallen asleep - I tiptoed over to the door - I listened - would you believe it Sean they were at it again!! - I should have known once isn't enough for the present generation of cybersexpots - it's all that herbal ecstasy they do - I looked at my watch: fuck it was 5 to 9!!! - with or without McS. I had to get back uptown - gleaming faintly in the moonlight beside her American Heart Assoc. pencil mug I spied Alice Worth's letter opener - I tried out the point on my palm - hmmm quite sharp - yes I thought with enough force and at very close quarters . . . I slipped it up my sleeve - I eased open Alice's desk drawer - Voilà! - a $20 clipped to a post-it marked STAMPS - thanks very much Alice this will get us back up to the Met - The uptown ride was fast - we avoided the construction this time - I got back just before the end of intermission: the lobby was packed - punters huddled together in little clumps: oh yes oh yes fabulous I heard her at Bayreuth in '93 wonderful just wonderful nodding their stuffed heads fingering their Callas amulets - I pushed through the lowing herd my eyes raking the room for Peter and party - a security wallah was talking to a big guy in a tux - the midget vampire was circulating hitting his little xylophone - Time it's time - but where was Pierre and Co.? - fuck fuck fuck what if they went in already?? - but a moment later I found myself standing right behind them - from L to R: the old granny - she was leaning on Peter's arm - the Clown-Spouse - Le Boy - Forveaux was only inches away I could have stretched out and grabbed a fistful of grey swinger locks I could have bitten the boy's neck and goosed the old lady under her fur coat - monsieur le rapiste et famille were heading back around the corner for Act 2 or whatever it was - suddenly Alice's letter opener came to life - it slithered down my shirt sleeve and into my grip - the crucial question was could I find his black heart from behind with one stab? I wouldn't get a second chance - I think I was just about to lunge at him when Le Boy turned to the Clown-Spouse and said: What night is Glock?

CLOWN-SPOUSE (indeterminate foreign accent): Glock? Which one?

LE BOY: *The Water Sprite*

CLOWN SPOUSE: *The Water Sprite*? I don't know . . . Isn't it Thursday? (consults her programme) No. Thursday is Berlioz. *Beatrice et Benedict* . . .

FORVEAUX (with finality): We are going to see *The Water Sprite* next Monday

Next Monday - *The Water Sprite* - thank you Peter - I let them go in - I stood and watched them climb the stairs - Pierre was helping the granny - till Monday then - enjoy the show - SNUFFOUT is go - I headed for the exit - right beside the door Sean mounted on an easel there was a big colour poster of King Neptune brandishing his trident riding in a seashell chariot pulled by rearing seahorses and underneath

THE WATER SPRITE
(Der Wassergeist)
W.W. Glock
Mon 27th - Wed 29th - Thur 30th January
8 P.M.

All at once Sean a shiver ran down my spine: I'd remembered my I-Ching readout

The man enters the watery cavern

I'm a rock and jazz cat Sean I don't pretend to know the first thing about opera but I *do* know that any opera called *The Water Sprite* is bound to have an act probably Act 2 set in a watery cavern / a cavern under the sea with a backdrop of painted seaweed and a coral throne for King Neptune to park his fat tenor bottom on or else by the law harry this isn't the end of the 18th century and my name isn't

·133·

Wolfgang Wilibeard Glock (b. Detmold 1717 d. insane London 1771 thinking he was a fox terrier - I looked him up in the Camb. Bio. Dic) - I knew it Sean I knew it in my gut the moment I saw Pierre go into the Met I said to myself this feels right this is the place where we do our dance - Glock is The Word

——•——

Look to your laurels Jan Svankmajer - bow down ye Quays and Katsuhiros - kick-started by the Lincoln Center Breakthrough my creative juices have started to FLOOOW: 'DIE FROG DIE!' is the name of the new product - 'an animated masterpiece' rave Seebert and Eggbert '3 thumbs WAY UP!' - Casting Notes: Gary Oldman will play Bartlett O'Plantagenet (the ME character) - Everyone else is a puppet / cel / claymation except the pivotal Amelia-stripper-undercover-cop character played by Lisa Marie - or Heather Graham?? - WHY NOT BOTH!!? = my homage to Buñuel!

THE GHOST PARADE SCENE - Background: One Sunday afternoon last summer terribly hung over I ran slap bang into not 1 but 2 parades of national identity: coming at me down 5th Ave. was the Korean National Day Parade - one block over marching up 6th the Poles were celebrating their mystic Polishness - I spent an hour skipping back and forth between them digging the sights and sounds - Polish High Point: dozens of blond 17 yr. old ice maiden perfect 10s wandering around all wearing MISS POLONIA sashes - everyone's a winner baby that's for sure - Korean High Point: The Mother Carboneri High School Marching Band with the girls in their short-short electric blue jail-bait-and-proud-of-it skirts white gogo boots tight tunics with gold piping tall *Nutcracker* hats w/ pink and blue plumes some playing portable glockenspiels!!!- and what tune was it? - none other than that perennial marching band staple 'Every Move You Make' by The Police A.K.A. The Stalkers' National

Anthem - 5 minutes later hanging with the Poles I was watching the so-and-so high school band from Boonton NJ march by - and what were they playing? - I kid you not it was the BAGPIPE VERSION of that self-same dreadful tune!!! - In my movie O'Plantagenet is in the crowd watching the parade - the band's playing 'Every Move' - he's humming along every move you make every breath you take - suddenly he sees Amelia's Ghost - she's one of the drum majorettes - she winks at him as they march by and of course he receives it - the wink / the song / her ghostly presence - as a flaming epiphany / 3 thumbs way up from the Norns that he's on the right track - 'Power-ful' - 'Compelling' - 'DIE FROG DIE! is a must see'

———•———

1/22 5.30 A.M.: At first I imagined myself carrying out the execution *inside* the auditorium - after plugging Peter I'd leap onto the stage à la Wilkes Booth croon a few bars of 'That Old Black Magic' or 'Unfor-gettable' and then blow my brains out before the security goons could lay a finger on me - this scenario went down in flames when I called the box office to score a ticket for the Monday night - they're COM-PLETELY SOLD OUT which I should have foreseen because accord-ing to today's *Times* W. W. Glock - for so long shamefully neglected blah blah - is currently enjoying an exciting posthumous critical revival etc. thanks in no small part to a 'sparkling' new critical bio of the mad Detmolder penned by his great great great great grandson a fat grinning long-haired music bore from Wien plus they've just come out with a 6 CD box set of all his symphonies conducted by Herbert von Collabo so in other words Wolfgang Wilibeard you are THE MAN right now and tickets for your *Water Sprite* are not to be had for love nor $$$ - I asked about standing room - I asked about last minute cancellations - the condescending moron at the other end kept stringing me along: well sir if you would like to call back on the night of the performance we may be able to accommodate you blah blah - I hung up on him: anyway scoring a ticket is completely pointless because I don't have the foggiest where Peter & Co. are sitting!!!! - So we're back out in the lobby - and a very good thing too because it really is the only place to do it and get away with it - (scratch what I said about blowing my brains out - I was having a romantic moment - remember Poe: 'a wrong is not redresseth if retribution slamdunketh the redresser') - I double checked the start time: kick off is at 8 - I don't know if you're familiar with Glock's operatic works Sean - he wrote 11 in all as well as symphonies and concertos and chamber music and at least 75 long-winded fan letters to Swedenborg - the Mystic Swede never wrote back - this from Cox & Scofield's *Guide to the Opera* 12th ed:

'Gorgias, a water sprite, learns that his daughter Arethusa has fallen in love with Rudolfo, a simple shepherd. Helped by the King of the River, Gorgias hatches a plan . . .'

but first you can be very sure he goes on about it for half an hour

Oh

woe

is me

My daughter loves a mortal man

My daughter loves a mortal man

My daughter loves a more

ah-more-ah-more

ah-more-ah-more

ah-more-ah-MORE-

tilllllllll

man

(Chorus: O woe is he! His daughter loves a mortal man etc.)

1/22 8 A.M.: Ahoy there Sean I'm going back up to the Met tonight to case the joint properly - Report to follow

---

1/22 11 P.M.: MET CASING REPORT : single most valuable piece of info gleaned = something I completely overlooked!!! = there's ANOTHER revolving doors way down at the far end of the lobby - not many punters know about it / use it / but a few do - so Peter & Co. *might* enter that way - they've probably bought their tickets already so there's no reason for them to go anywhere near the ticket windows i.e. the part of the lobby where I saw them on Monday - Conclusion: There's only one place to hang and have ALL entrances covered and that's right in front of the ticket takers - the big plus about waiting for Peter here is that the security wallahs tend to hover around the box office i.e. I notice they don't poke their heads around the pillar too much - however there's a possible large minus in the shape of 2 guys in tuxes who stand facing the ticket lines - both are big and beefy - one of them looks like a retired boxer shaved head broken nose cauliflower ear he never stopped whistling classical favourites all the time I was standing there - he's big but he looks like he could really move if he had to - clearly the antidote to arousing the tux guys' suspicions is to be VERY WELL TURNED OUT which means no unsightly McSplatter bulges / calm cool collected / radiating a patrician 'I own the place' vibe: Who me? I'm just standing here waiting for my wife to come back from the powder room - act the part and they'll leave you alone - NB NB: 2nd MOST VALUABLE INSIGHT: by 7:25 the lines to go in are already forming - To be absolutely sure I don't miss them I have to be in position by 7 at the latest - Sean has a question - yes Sean? - why not keep watch outside his office and follow him up to the Met in a cab? - A: yes Sean that *would* be the way to go except for one thing: Suppose the old granny suddenly takes ill? - she gets all anxious and agitated about going to see a Glock opera on a Monday night in January - it's a Parisian thing you wouldn't understand - or call it a premonition - and so Pierre has to stay home from work on the Monday and sprinkle her with eau de cologne and read Victor Hugo to her to calm her down - No Sean to be absolutely 100% sure McSplatter and I must be there to greet la famille at the turnstiles

———•———

Thurs 23 / 2.20 A.M.: I almost forgot - you'll never believe who I saw when I was casing the Met yesterday - MARTHA !!!! - yes Sean Martha my estranged wife - Sean (jaw drops open): you met Martha at the Met? But what an extraordinary coincidence! - I know - it's very weird - but you see it just so happens Martha was visiting Lincoln Center yesterday with her class - her Gifted Group - you don't know her Gifted Group? - oh she's very proud of them - they're a bunch of genius kids - 7th graders all with skyrocket IQs - the pride of Alexander Hamilton High where she's teaching at the moment - anyway Martha and her class were on a tour of Lincoln Center - I was plotting my escape route when suddenly they came pouring into the lobby - Martha and 20 of her students - they didn't see me because I saw them first and nipped behind the big pillar - they formed a circle around Martha by the 1st ticket window and she proceeded to recount the history of the Met recalling some of the great throats who'd sung there Kiri Te-Kanawa - Placido - John McCormack - Bono - Cathy 'One Roulade' Berberian - Matt Monro - Roy Rodgers and Trigger - anyway this nice-looking elderly couple - clearly out-of-towners - happened to come walking by and the old man got talking to one of the gifted kids - the old lady beamed at the children and beamed at Martha and said they looked to be very good children indeed - at which point one of the kids a girl of with coke bottle glasses freckles and braids piped up:

- Please Miss Suarez please may we sing our special song for this nice old lady and gentleman?

- Please Miss Suarez! came a chorus of eager young voices around her - Please Miss Suarez! Let us sing our special song!

At first Martha said no - she told them singing probably wasn't allowed in the lobby of the Met - the kids were crushed - they uttered a collective moan - the old couple were crushed too - but then one of the security guards stepped forward and smiled and winked and said it's OK the big boss ain't around go ahead knock yourselves out - well the kids and the old folks were overjoyed - the old couple sat down on folding canvas picnic chairs and the kids quickly lined up in front of them like a proper school choir with Martha facing them as their choral conductor - then the glasses-and-braids kid stepped forward and made a charming curtsy to the old folks:

- This song is called 'The Ballad of Pierre Forveaux' she announced. It's a group composition by the kids of Miss Suarez's Special Advanced Class at Alexander Hamilton High. We hope you will enjoy it - Then Martha raised her arms - she gave a nod to the security guard - he was standing off to one side all set to accompany them on Kurt Weil sinister sea shanty accordion - and the kids started singing

> *Pierre Forveaux had Wealth and Power*
> *But Something was troubling him.*
> *He was known as a witty bon vivant*
> *Till his face grew dark and grim.*

His friends said 'Peter, tell us what's wrong.'
Pierre's lawyer's lip did curl:
'Mon dieu, mon dieu, she is killing me.
I must 'ave zat lissel girl.'

'Which little girl?' his friends inquired
'Do you mean Lilly White's new bonne?'
'Damn your eyes,' the lawyer snarled
'I'm in thrall to la belle Yvonne.'

'But Yvonne is your own stepdaughter!
And she's not yet turned thirteen!
Denied the love of a faery child
Would you morph into Mr. Mean?'

They agreed 'He needs distraction.
There's plenty more flesh in the sea.'
'But I'll never know joy,' Pierre did moan
'Till Yvonne's in the sack with me!'

Well they took him out for some gourmet sex
To the best whorehouse in town
The madam gave them the run of the house
And they proceeded to bust some moves.

They brought him twins from old San Juan
They gave him the Bangkok Twirl
But Peter sighed 'I am bored, so bored.
I must 'ave zat lissel girl.'

Suddenly and unaccountable The Gifted Group skipped ahead to
Verse 41:

He cornered Yvonne one moonless night
When no one was around
She fought him off and ran outside
In a red silk dressing gown . . .

All right Sean I confess - you've probably guessed by now that I DIDN'T see Martha and her Gifted Group at the Met - I made the whole thing up - Prendergast de Jarelay is le vrai balladeer - shall I spin it out for another 90 verses? - nothing easier - Here's the plot: Forveaux rapes Amelia - 10 yrs go by - I meet her and fall in love - Martha kicks me out - Amelia dumps me - Prendy buys a gun and goes looking for Peter - Amelia offs herself - my Kamikaze Mourning Period - Reunion with Martha - enter Dame Raptor - Martha kicks me out AGAIN - My Homelessness - I am cruelly cheated out of my Inheritance - The Insulting Teapot - My Descent into Despair - I meet Stephanie the drunken temp - The Birchmont Epiphany - establishment of the Command Post - Prendy stalks Forveaux - The Lincoln Center Breakthrough - verse by gripping verse Sean I'll hold my listeners spellbound as I spin the tale right up to the present moment - up to Peter's Execution and Beyond - 98 or 298 verses - I'd call it a not unworthy addition to the genre and of course it's going to be heavily featured on the soundtrack of DIE FROG DIE! - but if I want to do this right I'm going to have to get more booze - here Sean take this fistful of glowing green ghost money - see what you can rustle up for us on the mean streets of St. Rudysburg

————•————

THURS 23: Ah me Sean how the great wheel turns - One minute everything's going swimmingly Lady Luck's standing behind your chair in a low-cut evening gown massaging your shoulders nibbling your earlobe go baby go and the next minute she's gone - pouf - the World Horse (Die Welthoss) is shot right out from under you and you're back down rolling around in the dust and the muck - barely 36 hrs after the Lincoln Center Breakthrough the Norns unleashed the fury of hell's darkest pit straight at my throat - the trouble started last night: there I was toiling away in the wee wee hours on The Ballad of Pierre Forveaux - I knocked out another 40 verses Sean remind me to show them to you - suddenly it hit me: you eejit Prendergast you have to ERASE the Dossier of the Accused stuff off Vincent's hard-drive IMMEDIATELY!!!! = pages and pages of incriminating shit!!! - clickety-click-click - delete delete delete - it didn't take long - I was feeling relieved and very pleased with myself - crisis averted etc. - and of course that's when things start to go wrong - when you're feeling good - I decided to kick back and relax but Self-Indulgence got the upper hand . . . and so it came to pass Sean the very thing we've been dreading: it was like the recurring nightmare I told you about except instead of being curled up in the sleeping bag I was on the floor near the front door - I opened my eyes - it was morning - Vincent and Robbie the Robot were staring down at me - I followed their gaze - I was in my birthday suit - no time to ponder how or why - I immediately launched into my explanation: Oh Mr. Szabo there you are! I suddenly felt dizzy etc.- No go: Vincent started hitting me with his umbrella - I rolled out of reach - he came after me yelling and swinging - I retreated on all fours - Robbie was halfheartedly trying to hold him back but Vincent was livid Sean more livid than I've ever seen him - his face was brick red and there were little grey steam jets coming out his nostrils - as I crouched behind the big Minolta he exploded into the mother of all tongue lashings: How dare you - taking advantage of my good nature - your surly attitude - alienating the customers - I gave you too many chances blah blah blah - betraying my trust (what trust??!) - all the time he was shaking his brolly in my face - to add fuel to the fire Robbie announced the discovery of my sleeping bag and clothes on the couch - they went through my trouser pockets and

found the store keys - Vincent: How long have you been living here?
TELL ME HOW LONG YOU'VE BEEN LIVING HERE! - no way
José zip the lip I wasn't going to tell him anything - of course this
prompted them to conduct The Big Search: in next to no time they'd
tumbled the rest of my stuff including stalking suit shirts shoes etc.
- they found a couple of empty Jägermeister bottles beside the VCR
- that was the clincher - all that remained was for Judge Dred to don
the black cap and pronounce sentence: I was told I had 10 minutes
to quit Kwik forever - never darken my door etc. - then the righteous
one stomped off to buy his morning paper - a parting shot: you better
not be here when I get back Prendergast. If you are I'm calling the
police I mean it - yakety yak - paranoid old bollocks - Robbie was told
to oversee my pack up 'n' go - he hovered over me while I got dressed
watching me with his cold robot eyes - like I was going to sneak out
with a 4 ton copier in my knapsack! - I was stuffing my toiletries in a
plastic bag when my heart missed a beat: *McSplatter!* - McSplatter
was still asleep in his little hammock under the couch!! - how on earth
was I going to distract Robbie long enough to effect the retrieval of my
weapon??? - In answer to my prayer the phone rang - Robbie picked
up: Good morning Vincent's Kwik Copy may I help you? - I'm sure he
had every intention of keeping an eye on me as per instructions but
it wasn't just anyone on the phone oh no it was beautiful Daisy Colon
The Foxy Queen of Kwik - it's well known that Robbie has a big crush
on her - the robot came to life: Daisy! What's up? - she was calling in
sick apparently - I began making hand gestures suggestive of coition -
Robbie flushed beetroot and turned away - Prendy sprang into action:
I dropped my can of shaving cream - oops! - which I promptly kicked
under the couch - I knelt and put my paw in under as if to get it and in
a few seconds McSplatter was free - quick down the front o' me troors
went Mr. Lethal Weapon - I straightened up and turned around -
Robbie was off the phone and glaring at me: Are you ready? - just

about I said - OK. Let's go - and so struggling unaided with knapsack dufflebag assorted plastic bags plus my suit slung over my shoulder I was escorted in silence to the front door and without so much as a good luck or a fare thee well the model worker held the door open I staggered through and he shut it behind me - So that was that: The End of Prendy's Stint at Kwik and good riddance - I threw my gear in a taxi and headed over to the storage hole - the NYU Radiosnothead at the desk had the audacity to tell me I'd have to rent another space for the new stuff - no fucking way sunshine I want to speak to your boss - the manager appeared a thin serious woman with dreads - I told her if they didn't let me put my suit and shoes etc. in with the rest of the stuff I'd take everything out - the bluff worked - the new shit was duly thrown in on top of the old and I exited head held high - Under normal circumstances I'd be worried about where I'm going to live: 1. I'm persona non gratia chez Privette - 2. My Williamsburg studio's out of bounds unless I want my goolies crushed by the Brothers O. - 3. the Bowery Mission's out because they search your bags - they're not supposed to but they do - 4. Raptor won't take me back (thank God) - happily these are NOT normal circs and upon reflection I see that my new homelessness actually dovetails perfectly with the mission: it's always a smart move to disappear just before you break the social contract because that way there's fewer clues / leads when they come after you - so from this day forth Prendy's blip will be off all radar screens - I intend to be a ghost of a shadow of a chimera Sean a vague clump of mist drifting beneath the castle walls at dawn - minimum visibility guarantees maximum impact - ONLY 5 DAYS TO SNUFF OUT!! - plenty of time to worry about mundane shit like where I'm going to live after the deed is done

————

Thurs 1/23 10 P.M.: Long Island City: I've had quite a day Sean - I spent the afternoon riding out to Canarsie back and forth on the L back and forth back and forth with McSplatter in my inside coat pocket - why Canarsie? - Why not? - I'm a free agent jobless homeless I can do what I want - when Martha and I were first married we had a chiropractor who lived out in Canarsie - a Dr. Reddich or Roddich a tall sardonic 55ish hipster Kurt Vonnegut lookalike - he smoked Chesterfields and was always humming Beatles tunes and glancing at you sardonically over the top of his tortoiseshells - one day in the middle of an adjustment he asked Martha to run away with him to Paraguay - she said no - Reddich then confessed that whenever she came to see him such was her beauty that afterwards he was forced to commit the sin of Onan - his exact words apparently - and having made his confession the naughty malpractor walked out of his examination room humming 'Love Me Do' - of course Martha was extremely freaked out - she got dressed quickly and left the foul fiend's house - the next day I drove out to Canarsie to confront him - we had a heated exchange in the waiting room - he denied making improper advances - you and your wife both need your heads examined - oh really? Is that so? - I unhooked his display skeleton from the stand and started dancing around the waiting room with it singing 'Mean Mr. Mustard' - at Roddich's prompting the receptionist picked up the phone to dial 911 but I dumped Mr. Bones on her head dashed outside and leapt into the Charger - in those days I ruled the road in a 1970 Dodge Charger - I sped away . . . and 10 yrs later there I was riding out to Canarsie on the L thinking about Martha and Arthur (?) Roddich a man with big warm hands who loved her or at any rate had the hots for her - suddenly I remembered something crucial: my execution kit was incomplete - tut tut Sean you were supposed to remind me: I need to buy a silencer for McSplatter!!! - A Silencer - O sacred object from childhood! - you couldn't be a true fan of 007 and the Man from U.N.C.L.E. and not be into silencers - There and then I decided to return to Long Island City and buy one from the old gun seller - Eastern Parkway was coming up a creepy crisscross junction in the middle of burnt-out Bklyn - I got off the train - for some reason I was sure Long Island City was in Brooklyn - of course it's not it's in Queens - evidence of how fucked up the NY subway system is: to get to Queens I had to take the J all the way back into Manhattan and then stay on it while it looped back out to Brooklyn again - at DeKalb I boarded a northbound N - I endured an endless crawl back up through Manhattan in sardine can rush hr. conditions replete with musical beggars - This little light of mine / I'm gonna let it shine / up your arse - orthodox women in wigs howling hellspawn in strollers subnormal dishwashers reading derivative comic books and blond Wall St. yuppies staring into space mentally boffing their stepmothers - it took us 45 minutes to get to Queens - I got off at the B'way stop - I walked down the stairs onto the street - it was dark and cold and starting to rain - How was I going to find the old man's gun shop? - try as I might I couldn't remember the name of it or what street he was on (12th Ave?? 11th St.?) - I remember it had a weird name i.e. it wasn't anything obvious like So-and-So's Hand Guns or Jim Jones & Co. Rifle Shop - it was something like Franz Josef Discount Foam and Bedding - I remembered he also sold things like water mattresses and beepers and radar detectors - I was walking down B'way racking my brains - I saw a diner and went in and ordered a cup of coffee - I asked the man behind the counter if I could have a peep at his Yellow Pages - he jerked his head towards the back - there was a phone on the wall beside the gents - I pulled my old friend the YPs off the little undershelf and started thumbing - I couldn't even sit down with it they'd chained it to the wall - I found GUNS & GUNSMITHS and started going down the list: Alpine Taxidermy in College Point . . . Aqua Pet Hobby Den in Flushing . . . Bayside Whitestone Lumber—

- Hey you

I looked up: there was a very big big man towering over me - 6ft. 5 red complexion ginger moustache plaid jacket check shirt huge beer gut spilling out over his jeans - I immediately sensed danger in the puffy piglet eyes and jutting jaw - he pointed at the YPs and inquired with markedly slurred speech:

- what ya lookin' faw?

I'm looking for a good chiropractor I said. Do you know any? - he shook his head slowly and belched - his eyes rolled up into his head - for a second he seemed about to topple forward but instead he clamped one huge paw onto the booth behind him and steadied himself - I'd already eased the phone book back on to the shelf and was starting to edge around him - but he rotated his belly effectively blocking my escape - Scuse me I said - no response he just stood there swaying - I stared up at him - he glared down - impasse - all at once a strange light appeared in his eyes - he pointed at me:

- You - you ever have anal sex?

- Never. Please let me through. My wife is waiting for me out in the car

His eyes narrowed:

- Look I *know* you know about it

What to say? His inebriation might be feigned i.e. he might be the advance scout of a queer-bashing party or a religious nut who equated buggery with Satanism posing as a wrecked drunk in order to trap me into a vicious beating - I was itching to produce McSplatter and poke the barrel in his gut but instead I decided to go the friendly macho route: Hell yes I said. I've done it. I've done it hundreds of times. Always with the ladies of course. And you? - He grinned proudly: Last night. My girlfren' . . . She let me . . . My warmest congratulations I said and now if you'll excuse me - It's tight he continued. It's really tight. Like this - he grabbed my thumb in his clenched fist - This is what it feels like - He pulled his arm back and I was jerked forward - He bellowed in my ear: This is what it feels like! - It was a ridiculous situation - a drunken stranger had had an enjoyable sexual experience and in his eagerness to share he was squeezing all the blood out of my thumb - Help! I shouted Get him off me! Help! - the diner owner and a waitress came running - it took a full minute of tense negotiating but between them they persuaded Don - that was his name - to release me whereupon he staggered back and fell into one of the booths where he lay cursing and demanding beer while the waitress tried to soothe him - meanwhile the owner walked me to the door - he put a hand on my shoulder: I'm sorry about that. He's not a bad guy - It's his girlfriend I feel sorry for I said - Yeah I guess. Did you find what you were looking for? - What? - in the Yellow Pages? - oh yes thank you I lied and I pushed the door open and stepped back out into the night. At least the rain had eased off - I continued down Broadway - I was feeling very annoyed with myself Sean - I should have finished searching the YPs but I'd let Don derail me - evidently it was the Norns' will that I find the old man's shop without aid of map or compass - after many blocks I hit Vernon Blvd . . . soon I was lost in the industrial wasteland - 33rd Rd . . . 33rd Drive . . . 10th St . . . 11th Ave . . . I wandered up and down and back and forth across the grid . . . featureless warehouses . . . factories . . . it all looked the same . . . a couple of cranes stood idle against the night sky . . . I passed a parking lot full of cement mixers . . . I saw a stray dog or possibly a huge rat peeing on a heap of garbage in a vacant lot . . . at one point I had to step back into the shadows to avoid a gang of juvenile delinquents sauntering by in their puffy ski jackets - all the time I was trying to visualise the outside of the old man's gun shop - was it a storefront? did it have a sign? *Was* it in the industrial section? I wasn't sure any more - I thought I'd better find another coffee shop and consult the YPs again - or better still a nice warm bar - suddenly a gin and tonic seemed like an excellent idea - I turned a corner - and there he was!!!! - 40 yards away walking on the other side of the street outlined against a wall of corrugated iron - the stoop the shuffle the shock of white hair were unmistakable - I was about to shout Hey old man do you sell silencers but just then he disappeared around a corner - I sprinted after him - from around the corner came a sudden burst of sounds - shouts blows a ragged scream - I put on the breaks tiptoed to the corner poked my head around the corrugated - and drew back - it was the same gang of juves Sean - they were standing in a circle beating and kicking the old gun seller who lay moaning on the ground - I started to tiptoe away - but then up spake an inner voice: 'Remember You're Packing!' - a luxurious shiver ran down my spine - in the distance I heard the hunting horns of Sherwood Forest and then McSplatter himself addressed me in his Cagneyesque bark: waddaya waitin for? Get out there and teach dem goddam punks a lesson - and so rashly jeopardizing SNUFFOUT for a cheap thrill I stepped out of the shadows and hailed the 6 bad boys:

- Police! Freeze!

They stopped what they were doing and turned towards me - I started walking towards them with McSplatter pointed skywards - when I was about 10 ft. away I fired twice in the air - BLAM BLAM - the shots were incredibly loud!!! - there was a moment of shocked silence followed by a chorus of oh shits then the young hoodlums took to their heels scrambling over one another to escape the righteous wrath of the Prendinator - with solemn glee I watched them legging it down the block - they disappeared around the corner - for half a minute I stood there savouring the stillness and feeling like Steve McQueen

- my reverie was interrupted by the groans of the victim on the ground
- I stuck McS. in my waistband and went up to him - there was blood
flowing freely from his nose and he had a big gash on his forehead - he
was bleeding from the mouth too - he'd lost some teeth - his little round
glasses lay on the ground beside him one of the lenses was smashed -
was he trying to speak? Yes - I bent closer - I heard a choked whisper

- Nein . . . Nein . . . Meine Kinder . . . Meine Kinder . . . Nein—!

I stared down at him - any minute there'd be cop car sirens and
ambulances and I'd have to run - I looked up and down the street - not
a soul - I knelt down and started patting his pockets - I freely admit
Sean I was out of my mind I didn't really know what I was doing - he
gave a little groan - sorry mate - I pulled his wallet out of his trouser
pocket - banknotes - credit cards - bus pass - NYC library card - his
green card! - JASZCHUK, HENDRYK BOLESLAW / D.O.B. 03-21-
27 / Alien Number AO29501537 - and yes here it is pay dirt: half a doz.
little business cards with the shop address on them! - suddenly old
Hendryk sat up - his fingers clamped on my arm like a vice - his eyes
opened wide and he stared up at me - I think he must have recognised
me his gun-crazed son-surrogate because he almost smiled - then a
terrible shudder ran through his frame and he slumped back - dead
weight - finito - shit! - I was still holding his wallet - I looked around:
the street was deserted - I stuffed the wallet back in his jacket - then
I took it out again - it was covered with my prints what was I thinking
of ??!! - I took out the banknotes and stuffed them in my pocket then
I put the wallet in my coat pocket - I'd just taken a bunch of keys out
of his trousers when I saw car headlights - 4 or 5 blocks away a car
was turning on to the street - I jammed the keys in my pocket and
ran back around the corner

At this moment I'm lying on Hendryk Jaszchuk's big brass bed - ironically HENDRICK'S SPORT & HOBBYS (sic) is only 2 blocks from where the owner breathed his last - the apt. is right over the shop - it's a quiet street and I don't think my entry was observed - I can't make up my mind if Hendryk was a bachelor or a widower: there's a framed picture in the living room of a rather attractive blonde in her 30s (?) with a 1940s hairdo - Mrs. Jaszchuk? an old flame? a favourite sister?? - anyway she's not here tonight - I'm happy to report there are no cats or dogs or hamsters or canaries on the premises - I'm completely alone - I know what you're thinking Sean: 'Prendergast have you taken leave of your senses? Don't you realise that once they identify the body the police will make a beeline for the old man's shop?' - point taken - I'm not saying being here isn't risky - you might say *very* risky - on the other hand it's only been 3 hrs since the murder - I bet you anything they won't identify him for several days - I have his wallet remember - if and when the cops bust in I'll simply pretend I'm Jaszchuk's idiot son Jerzy IQ 74 deaf and dumb since boyhood thanks to a vicious blow from a Red Army rifle butt during the riots in the Old Town Square in '54 - 'You little prick I'll teach you to throw stones at a Soviet tankist!' - Seriously if they *do* bust in I'm up and away over the roofs - I've sniffed out an unlocked roof door 2 buildings over - I toyed briefly with the idea of hanging a sign on the door of the shop GONE BACK TO OLD COUNTRY SIGNED THE MANAGEMENT to deter customers / nosey neighbours etc. - at first it seemed like a good idea but on second thoughts it would only enflame the snoopers' curiosity - instead what I have to do is lie low keep the curtains drawn and go on tiptoe - shades of my former garage life except Chez Jaszchuk definitely has a lot more perks: The big brass bed = very comfy - The fridge = well stocked with sausages rashers milk beer etc. - A perfectly charming ancient wooden cuckoo clock on the wall behind the telly - several bottles of quality schnapps - a little while ago I had a rummage around downstairs: I found a cardboard box literally jampacked with silencers - 2 of them fit McSplatter like a glove so Mission Accomplished - Snuffout Kit es perfecto - it's time for a hearty mug of schnapps

———•———

1/24 / 2 P.M.: - Made a sortie into Manhattan this morning to get MY DISGUISE - to be on the safe side I made it a 6 A.M. exit via the back door - quick jog through the back lot out onto the street - along Vernon Blvd - back up Broadway - hopped on the N - I was first customer of the day at Gordon's the theatrical costumers on Lafayette - I tried on hundreds of beards and false noses - in the end I bought a light brown wig & matching moustache - top class workmanship - they both look amazingly realistic - after Gordon's I hit the storage hole and grabbed my Execution Suit and my CD player - coming back half asleep on the train I happened to see a headline in the paper QUEENS HIT AND RUN MYSTERY MAN - what's this? what's this? - Trying to read over the guy's shoulder: 'Long Island City . . . 11th Ave . . . Late Thursday night . . . No witnesses . . .' It had to be Jaszchuk! - 'the skull . . . completely crushed . . . making identification difficult if not impossible . . .' - after I left him Sean it seems some heartless bastards ran over him in a car - or possibly a truck - my God it really wasn't his night the poor old fuck - I take the crushed skull as a sign that there's no going back - that the Norns are telling me to stay put in the shop till the deed is done - Evidence in support of this: there hasn't been one customer since I got here - a lot of his shelves are bare - it all points to Hendryk being semi-shut down / retired - the gun museum's certainly not what it was 3 yrs ago: most of the cases are empty - all the good stuff's gone - the Greeks are in accord: 'Stay where you are' - aye aye 10-4 roger and out - time for some schnapps

———•———

Hendrick's Sport and Hobbys Sat. Jan. 25th 6:15 P.M.: SNUFFOUT = minus 50 hrs and counting - we're almost there Sean: I feel good I feel positive - it's like being in training for the New York City Marathon: you don't want to peak too soon / you want to hit it just right - to psych up the killer in me I've been listening to one of my Top 10 favourite CDs of the '90s: SHAOLIN TEMPLE GUARDS' SPIRIT OF THE MOTHERF******G BEEHIVE - I'm sucking up energy and conviction and focus from the Zen Knights of Richmond Ave. - word - others sit around praying for their 2nd album but not this boy: Prendy's down deep in the groove headphones strapped upside my head jammin' with my homies Dinero Filthy Old Fucker Wok Killer Serious Buttman Mr. Curious Yeller and the rest of the bad-ass Temple Guard posse as they wail and rail and rant and rave on this their classic debut from '91 the groundbreaking *Beehive*:

> you stinking motherfuckas in your whitebread nation
> addicted to pornography and greed and masturbation
> when I blow up your house I'm gonna feel elation
> suck my dick motherfuckas - we invite litigation

Who would have dreamt that a 37 yr old European intellectual like myself could find solace and uplift in the violent rhymes and rhythms pumping out of the projects and back alleys of NYC's neglected '5th Borough'!? - Life is strange Sean and tonight with The Big Payback almost upon us I want to send PEACE and RESPECT to the Noble Knights of Shaolin Temple

Technique Number 2 for Fortifying My Resolve: I'm rereading Burroughs - bought a copy of *Naked Lunch* for 2 bucks yesterday - he's even better by flashlight! - one of the great scenes in world lit. is at the end when he kills the two narcotics agents - The importance of

being able to shoot left handed - My God fair fucks to you Bill Burroughs we shant see your like again - how old is he now? - He must
be 110 - I stopped off in Lawrence Kansas once to pay my respects
- we were limping back east on the last leg of the ill-fated Cum Jerks
Tour of North America - I wanted to pay homage to the Cat in the
Hat - I wanted to shake the paw touched by the savage God - me and
a million other virus-vectors - I got his address from a dishwasher
in the cafeteria at the university - we actually found his house but of
course he wasn't home: the old arse bandit was off out in the desert
somewhere shooting up bug spray with 2-headed emissaries from
Alpha Centuri and rogering their glowing behinds

———

Jan 26 / 9 A.M.: Very weird: early this morning I was shocked awake
by the sound of someone banging on the downstairs door - I got up
and peeped through the curtains - it was still dark outside / the angle
was too steep I couldn't see who it was - the hammering continued
- after a couple of minutes it stopped and the person stepped back
- it was an old woman Sean - she stood there in the dim dawn light
squinted up at the 2nd floor window - I shrank back - she shouted
something up in a foreign language and then went back to attacking
the door - she was a really old woman all dressed in black including
her headscarf and get this: *she was carrying a green milk churn*
- after about 10 minutes she gave up and went away - I watched her
out of sight - that's right old hag limp away back to your fairy fort
- we don't want any goat cheese today - I really don't know what to
make of it Sean - was it a bona fide visitation from the other world?
or merely one of Jaszchuk's superannuated gal pals looking for some
touch? - a green milk churn - symbol of what?

———

Sun. Jan 26. 4 P.M.: Brace yourself Sean I've had ANOTHER visitor: this time a World Famous Rap Musician has taken time out from his busy recording and touring schedule to drop by and offer yours truly some words of advice and encouragement - Here's what went down:

- Yo. Anybody home?

- Who's that?

- Filthy Old Fucker. Filthy Old Fucker from Shaolin Temple. I'm coming to you live inside your mind by the power of wushu mental telepathy. I'm here to let you know that the Temple Guards are down with you Trendy P

- Thanks FOF

- don't mention it 'cos word is you're carrying the weight of the world on your shoulders

- I am

- Trendy P I look at you - I look at you with your scrawny chicken chest and your scrawny shoulders all acne 'n' shit and no strength in your arms 'cos you don't work out son and you're drinking too much and you're smoking weed and you're living in a dead guy's house and it's dusty and damp it's bad for your asthma and you can't light the lamp you could get pneumonia and you *do* have insomnia and now you're hearing voices which tells me your mental mainframe is starting to crack you know what I'm saying and I ask myself is he going to be able to make this hit? The Temple Guards are worried about you

- I'm deeply touched

- Fuck that shit. Trendy P this is your chance to do something good for once. Don't fuck up. Peace

---

MONDAY 27TH JANUARY - 3 a.m. THIS IS IT: JARLETH L. PRENDERGAST IN ASSOCIATION WITH ARTAUD'S HIDING IN THE FOREST WITH A BOW & ARROW PRODUCTIONS PROUDLY PRESENTS

DIE FROG DIE!

or

PIERRE FORVEAUX'S LAST DAY ON EARTH

To hell with sleep sleep is out the window a round of schnapps for the home team - this is it Sean - the FINAL COUNTDOWN - for the time is upon us when all wrongs shall be righted and old scores settled - the Scales of Justice are about to tip - Laze duh on-ore sonn mas key diveen-ass laze as the Spaniards say - aye Tashtego his spout is a big one he fantails like a split jib in a squall - HA HA HA a pint under me belt I feel no pain - since you've been goh-hon I stay in the tavern EV-A-REE NIGHT I don't know karate but I know kaRAZA so come on feel the noize girls grab your dicks for the time fast approaches for you to dance with the grim reaper you lousy stinking bastard Forveaux I'll follow your casket on a pale afternoon and pelt it with dead cats come out you black and tans come out and fight me like a man she's not a girl who misses much I feel no pain Sean no pain at all HA HA HA a pint of schnapps you old stiff

---

BETRAYED

This is a dark day Sean the day dark the mind dark the heart shrivelled in the breast - I feel like one of our famous compatriot's fizzles

that running track down in hell made of dead leaves

Betrayed Sean we were betrayed - all that planning and prep and mental discipline it all came to nothing - I still can't believe what went down - I feel like a busted watch spring I'm numb blood turned to dish water a broken doll - Perfidy you won

All right - just for the record - here's what happened:

At the last moment I decided not to cab it to the execution site - instead I thought I'd better lose my face in the crowd - I boarded the uptown number 1 - got off at 66th - followed the signs for Lincoln Center - swathe in NYC anonymity the Man of Dark Purpose blent with the uptown artsy evening commuters Julliard babes w/ cello cases etc. - there was a guy playing the violin in a long leather coat on the downtown platform - it seemed a good omen - I exited the subway - walked down a long corridor - the click and clacking of the high-heel shoe - 2nd corridor: big posters for City Opera shows etc. - car park / garage on right = N.B. A BIG COP HANGOUT pray you avoid it - I followed the sign for 'Main Box Office' - through some glass doors - got on the escalator - and stepped off in the lobby of the Metropolitan Opera - ticket windows on right - gift shop behind me - ahead: revolving doors / glass doors / exit to front sq.- Time: 6:35 - only a few people around - I strolled past the security wallahs in my wig and 'tash - McSplatter with cold-war East German silencer attached concealed under trench coat draped over my right arm - past the ticket windows round the corner and into position opposite the ticket takers - 5 of them standing in a line all in their stupid Drac capes - I looked right I looked left: yes I had an unobstructed view of all the doors - one of the house managers walked by - no sign of the other one the retired boxer - 6:55 - I prayed the old lady Granny Forveaux was coming - she'd slow down Pierre and give me time to get in close - 7:10: punters were starting to trickle in - my God I thought what if a small child some sort of mutant with x-ray vision comes skipping by? - He stops in front of me - stares - his eyes widen - he runs back to his mother - he's tugging at her sleeve pointing: Mommy Mommy that man has a .38 Smith & Wesson concealed under his coat! - 7:20: lots of people milling around queuing up / going in - out of nowhere the old boxer appeared - of course he planted himself right beside me - he was barely 2 ft. away whistling arias and looking around - I started to sweat - relief: he moved off to talk to someone - suddenly I felt my 'tash slowly coming unstuck on the left side - I pressed it down - 7:30: still no sign of them - I was thinking God I really need to pee when

- Jarleth?

Don't turn your head - don't move a muscle

- Jarleth Prendergast?

a Dublin accent

- It fucking IS you you bastard!

Before me stood a total stranger - medium height stocky with a pudgy pale face 30something long curly black hair heavy-lidded antisocial eyes jet black eyebrows - he was staring at me grinning - he had bad teeth - very bad teeth . . . Suddenly with sinking heart I remembered him: Emmet Crannock - opinionated weekend punk from Stillorgan - back in '81 he sold me an oz. of speed that was mostly Johnson's baby powder - he used to pester my cousin Thelma hoping she'd do the dirty boogie with him but smart girl she told him to shove off - shove off Crannock - fighting down my mounting panic I stared at this ghost from the past this vile residue - with a supreme effort of will I looked him straight in the eye and replied in an exaggeratedly nasal American accent

- Sarry. Yuh gat the wrang guy

For a few seconds I saw doubt flicker in his eyes:

- Get the fuck! You're Jarleth Prendergast. I'd know you anywhere! Are you going in? What the fuck are you doing dressed up like that for ya bollix?

Blot him out - don't panic - focus on Forveaux - look right look left look right again

- Come on stop arsing around. I fucking know it's you. Look I'm not moving till you tell me why you're standing there with a false 'tash on. Eh? Hello?

Thou saucy knave! - tell me Sean how was I supposed to react? - I've lived through a lot recently: the shock of seeing Amelia's face on top of that piano - Losing my inheritance - Vincent busting me - countless evictions - finding the old gun seller nine tenths dead in the street - in short I think I know how to react in a crisis but this was different - this time the Norns had gone too far: where did they get off sending me this long-haired nit?? - 13 yrs since he last clapped eyes on me plus I'm heavily disguised AND HE STILL RECOGNISES ME?? - what the fuck was he doing in New York? - what the fuck was he doing at Lincoln Center on a Monday night?? - Since when had he sprouted high culture? a vulgar cretin who's idea of classical music was swallowing a lump of hash and prancing around to Depeche Mode! - I'm sorry Sean I lost my temper - Accident ... Coincidence ... I'm as ready as the next man to acknowledge the role Chance plays in our horrible lives but this was a low trick - a very low trick

I leaned forward and hissed in his ear:

- Listen to me Crannock I have a gun. Go away or I'll shoot you in the balls. I mean it. Turn around and start walking. Allez vite!

To underline my serious intent I gave him a sharp poke in the ribs with McSplatter - His mouth opened and closed he stared at me in disbelief but he did as he was told he walked away - no time to regret my outburst no time for second thoughts because moments later THERE THEY WERE coming towards me: Pierre and the old lady in front the Clown Spouse and Le Boy behind them with granny's bowlegg'd shuffle setting the pace - I glanced to my left: the old boxer was still talking to the other guy - all 5 ticket wallahs were engrossed in tearing tickets / passing punters through - I took a deep breath and started walking towards Forveaux - I was only 10 ft. away when I saw the cop - yes Sean one of New York's Finest was pushing towards us through the crowd - I could hear his radio crackling - in a flash I knew Crannock had betrayed me - he'd shopped me to the authorities like the weekend punk he was - but I didn't turn back Sean I want the record to show I kept on going - I shoved past a middle-aged couple and crossed to Peter's right - he was saying something to the Clown Spouse - now we were almost abreast - McSplatter was pointed at the big red X glowing over his heart - NOW - Goodbye You Bastard - I started to squeeze the trigger but suddenly my weapon was forced down - incredibly the little granny had sprung forward and locked her arms around my middle - my arms were pinned to my sides McSplatter was pointing at the floor her little head was thrown back

and her bony ravaged face was twitching - Au secours! Au secours!
she cried - I tried to step back but she clung like a barnacle - I tried
to bring the gun up but she squeezed me even tighter - the Clown
Spouse put a hand on her shoulder and said something to her in
French - for a split second I locked eyes with Forveaux - I know he
recognised me Sean I know he knew what was going down - I made
a supreme effort and my gun arm started to rise - but the old lady
was rising too clinging and rising - NOW - I squeezed off 2 rounds
- someone moaned - the granny let go and then I was running Sean
kicking and punching knocking punters down like bowling pins
sprinting towards the revolving doors at the far end of the lobby - go
serpentine go serpentine the army training I'd never had come back
to me - I knew the cop would be aiming for my legs but he didn't have
a clear shot because (a) the lobby was full of The Members of 13 and
(b) I was zigzagging / bobbing and weaving - WHUUMP - I collided
with the xylophone midget - he gave a terrified yelp - the stupid twit
clung to my lapel - I tried to hit him on the head with McSplatter
and somehow I dropped the gun - nothing to be done keep running
keep running - there were shouts and screams people diving to the
floor left and right - my wig was gone my 'tash was half off I jumped
Sean I sailed through the air crashed through the revolving doors
out on to the square running running with the NYPD the old boxer
the security guards Forveaux Le Boy and for all I know Leonard
Bernstein and the Count McCormack in hot pursuit - I dived down
some steps running towards Fordham University - I remember
thinking Fordham isn't that up in the Bronx but no it was Fordham
Law School how ironic to be running from the law towards a law
school I thought gasping for breath rolling and tumbling down hard
stone steps out on to the street then left left left my heart bursting
in my chest running towards the traffic and the lights expecting at
any moment the sting of cop lead searing through the back of my
calf a cab screeched to a halt I dived in and off we sped - Sean I take

it back all my bitter shallow words - THE NORNS RULE!! - for the man at the wheel was none other than my old friend Hoque Malibar - what are the odds?? etc. - I lay on the floor in the back of his yellow submarine gasping for breath gasping for breath - a hairy paw reached back through the hole in the glass - 4 thin fingers wiggled questioningly - I lobbed a wad of banknotes at him and in stoic silence Hoque drove me to safety - I shall never forget it Sean bombing down the West Side Highway coughing and gasping with that hot sweet Arab music pounding through the backseat yiddy yiddy yi yiddy yi yiddy yiddy yi yiddy yiddy yi yiddy yi yi yi

Prendy has been squished
O hear me
Prendy has been stepped on
by the blind camel of destiny

Martha was curled up on the couch reading - I took off my coat - Good evening Martha. It may interest you to know that I have just killed a man - She peered at me over the top of her specs: You have? Who? - A lawyer - pause - Why did you do that? - I killed him because he hath done grievous harm to one I love - Martha exhaled a blue cloud of Gitanes smoke and returned to her book . . . I sat in the kitchen drinking a tall glass of vodka . . . Otto was sound asleep on his pink cushion on the window sill . . . Père Gumby smiled down at me timidly from his coign of vantage on top of the fridge . . . after a while Martha's curiosity got the better of her: she said Jarleth do you mean it? You really killed someone? - Yes I said I really did - silence for a minute then she put her book down:

- my matador!

Smiling she held out her hand - I went over to her - she put out her cig and took off her specs and her trademark black turtleneck - then we made love Sean - It was fucking fantastic - Martha had discovered the killer in me and she liked it - she liked it a lot - It had been a long long time since we'd done the humpty hump - I came at last howling like a wounded animal shaking and bucking like a broken washing machine - Chalk one up for Trendy Prendy! Left the slave grinding at the mill! By George I feel better for that! etc. then I dissolved in tears - Martha held me close and stroked my hair and murmured sweet nothings in Spanish and puffed her cig over my head in the mellow afterglow - careful with that ash - the smell of French tobacco mixed not unpleasantly with the jungle scent of her armpits - I was drifting or so I imagined into a deep peaceful sleep when all at once there was a ferocious pounding on the door - POLICE OPEN UP! - Martha got up stubbed out her cig and called out: Just a minute. I'll be right there - Martha No! Please! Don't let them in! - Too late: there were fire axes tearing through the door . . . Radios crackling . . . Martha flashed me a sad sweet smile and opened the door - the cops poured in - they grabbed me maced me cuffed me . . . I was led away . . . of course Sean it was all a dream - a horrible wet dream - I woke up on the bench in the little park across from the United Nations cold and sick in semen-stained trousers shouting No Martha No

———·———

1/29 On The Run: called Privette this morning to negotiate an emergency loan - I have to get to Mexico or Canada - Maude answered - I hung up immediately - I'll try again later - things look bad Sean - I can't go back to the gun shop - I'd chance it if I hadn't dropped the gun in the lobby but by now they'll have traced McSplatter back to Jaszchuk - why didn't you use the loaf Jaraleet?- why didn't you file the serial number off you rank pathetic amateur??

———·———

1/29: Well Sean 'the fame that eluded him in life' etc.: I made the front page of this morning's *New York Post* (only p. 3 in the *Daily News*) - it's an old photo from c. 1990 and a very unflattering one at that - Martha must have given it to them - my hair's too long and I'm wearing a ridiculously tight-fitting leather jacket that I think belonged to Gary Jerk - I'm grinning like a fool and I have my arm around this big fat woman Clara who used to book the bands at the Viking Tavern on Bleeker St. where the Cum Jerks had a Wednesday night residency - I look insane and on drugs which of course is why they ran it - needless to say I'm totally misrepresented in the story - 'failed music promoter' indeed! - according to the *Post* I shot the old French lady through the left ankle - I was right: she *is* Forveaux's mother - sorry maman - they rushed her to St. Vincent's - she's described as 'recovering . . . not in danger' - I'm very relieved - after all it's not her fault that one of her brood turned out a wrong 'un - I want to send her a get-well card: 'Chère Madame Forveaux: I hope you feel better soon - please be assured that what happened was an accident - I had no intention of plugging you - I was aiming to squish one of your tadpoles - signed A. Wellwisher' - perhaps not

---

Are you watching Sean? - Are you keeping your high-powered binocs trained on me from the high ramparts of Solicitor Heaven? - Do you see them hunting Prendy like a dog? - see how they hound me through the friendless night? - I'm cold and hungry - I dodge down a side street - I double back - I filch a few scraps from a movie crew buffet parked on Mercer - it's Vienna 1948 - huge shadows on the wall - cobble stones - running running - there it is again that damn zither music - survival mantra: stay out of the sewers and the subway - hurrying at night through Chinatown down cold wide Allen Street - the bright red neon of the HO KONG S PERMARKE beckons - it's time to get those lights fixed boys . . . Now I'm in Central Park at dusk

- 2 sissy cops ride by on pushbikes - I dive into F.A.O. Schwartz - the giant 'funny' robot points his spanner arm at me and in a booming metallic voice accuses me of making a hames of the execution - my God Sean I *did* make a pig's arse of it didn't I? - My Epitaph: 'Setting out to right an unrightable wrong he shot an old French woman in the foot and was apprehended in a children's toy store after a short struggle' - I suppose with time off for good behaviour I could be out by 2020 - unless maman takes a turn for the worse and croaks in which case it's strap the matricide to the gurney and give him his lethal jab - grim scenarios both - If you walk far enough west on 40th St just before 10th Ave. you hit a bridge over a disused railway line - I spent last night hiding under there in the bushes - thanks to the hordes of rats and homeless people scurrying about I hardly slept a wink - I'm washed out Sean - there's nothing to be done there's nothing to be said - CRANNOCK TRAITOR BURN IN HELL

I saw it again - half an hour ago - the green Volvo ES 1800 - parked under a streetlamp like before but this time it was on Perry St in the West Village - when I saw it Sean I felt like crying - it's such a cool-looking little car - design brilliance winking at the world as if to say come on what are you waiting for? Hop in baby I'll carry you away over the border not a care in the world - there was nobody around so I moved in for a closer look - I leaned in to examine the dashboard - immediately flashing lights sirens klaxons EEE-AW EEE-AW RHAAR RHAAR RHAAR RHAAAR!! STAND BACK! PROTECTED BY GATOR! MOVE AWAY FROM THE VEHICLE! KEEP BACK 200 FEET! EE-AW EEE-AW WIRR WIRR RHAAR RHAAR RHAAR INTRUDER INTRUDER - that's the trouble with America Sean right there: the hysterical fixation with private property poisoning the dreams of the downtrodden masses

---

1/31 OH MR. PRENDERGAST YOU'RE A DESPERATE MAN: When fear grips the soul Sean we're driven to desperate measures: I found out that Raptor had moved to a doorman building on W. 18th - last night I decided to break into her apt. tie her up and hole up there till the heat dies down - so there I was at 8 o'clock this morning hiding behind a tree outside her place - after a few minutes out she came - and to my deep dismay Sean there was a hulking 6 ft. 9 in. muscle-bound colossus with her - he had a tanned and deeply stupid face with ridiculously chiselled features and a swept-back mane of shiny blonde hair - he looked like Fabio - Raptor appeared (there's no other word for it) radiant - She was gazing adoringly up at Mr. Muscles and he was gazing down at her with the exact same expression - in the midst of my thousand torments I experienced a painful green heart pang for one could tell at a glance that Gwyneth had found her Prince Charming or at least her Prince Biceps and that The Evil Ex (me) was totally forgotten and in time her and her Fabio would exchange badly designed engagement rings and mate and have platoons of happy stupid muscle-bound children - As I watched them walk off down the street hand in hand I knew I was sunk: I'd imagined her gagged and bound and stuffed in a closet but a 6 ft. 9 boyfriend with arms like tree trunks is something you don't want to mess with

———

Ladies and gennelmen please welcome . . . The 3 Stooges:

Here's Amelia Garrity - she's up on stage in some fleabag Jersey flesh pit junked up to the gills grinding her skinny butt in the customers' faces to 'Doll Parts' now and forever with a stoned smile on her face just about to unhook her bra - in her own mind's eye she's a pale corpse floating past my window Peter's window the customer's window with her long blue hair spread out on the water like a pillow - like that preraphaelite painting you see on book covers

Here's Le Frog sitting at his desk sipping his breakfast chocolat - he's looking out the window and starting to get a woody as he recalls the first time he had his inexcusable way with her - collabo artistes Maurice Chevalier and Arletty grind naughty parts above his head: your secret is safe with us mon vieux!

... and here am I the biggest fool of them all Jarleth Prendergast always just about to pull the trigger and shoot the little old lady in the foot - Au secours! Au secours! - and so it goes - around and afuckinground for all eternity ... ETERNAL RECURRENCE: Prussian nutjob F. Nietzsche was a sick puppy Sean but some of his ideas were right on the money

———

I dreamt I was back at Jaszchuk's - there was a knock at the door - I peeped through the chink - Aidan McGrath Esq. was standing out in the street squinting up at the building - the sun was glinting off his little round lawyer glasses - I went down and opened the door - he immediately grabbed my paw and congratulated me - he explained that Maxine and Bobbie were no more - the 2 old libertines had expired in grand style after a 6 day celebratory orgy out at the cottage in Howth - they'd indulged in too much slap and tickle with the hired help a troupe of exotic male dancers - both had made moving deathbed confessions each one fingering the other as the mastermind behind the scheme to cheat me out of my inheritance with a forged will - to cut a long story short McGrath had brought me my money at last - a cheque for $33,100 and another bonus one for $1,000,000 that I'd coincidentally won in the Irish Hospitals Sweepstakes - in he marched with a squad of Sweepstake nurses 6 big tall strapping country girls in their starched white nurses' uniforms - when I asked for my money McGrath immediately turned nasty and started to denounce me to the nurses in a bad French accent: 'Ziss man is za ringleezur. I 'ave proof that 'e plans to lead an army of ruseless mercenaries to Tibet to assassinate the Pope and the Dalai Lama and many 'oly monks - to mow zem down in cold blood on the streets of Lhasa with tommy guns!' - 'tommy guns' must have been a secret signal because suddenly with a great cry the nurses ripped off their uniforms - they now stood revealed as 6 big strapping Irish policemen - grinning McGrath peeled off his mask - it was my arch-enemy André Breton!! - at a nod from Breton the policemen produced knives and forks and spoons from their tunics and threw them in the air chanting VIVE DADA! DADA MO-MO KA-KA! - then one of them whacked me on the head with his truncheon - I went down - The scene shifted . . . I was on a windswept hilltop in ancient Greece - I turned around - Amelia was standing there dressed in Grecian robes like Isadora Duncan with a floral headband and crisscross sandals - she was glaring at me and holding a flowering tree branch which she shook at me accusingly - and all at once it hit me: I'd let her down

---

I let her down - yes I did - I botched the execution - we were face to face Sean he was only a foot away and I blew it - the only one who comes out of this smelling of roses is the old granny - amazingly fast reflexes and the heart of a lion - they should give her the Legion of Honour - who touches a hair of yon grey head etc. - but what of Jarleth Prendergast Failed Assassin? - well for him Sean it's The Dark Night of the Soul - tableau: the hunter flees through the dark forest pursued by the blackbirds of regret - the reality is The Little Freak is long dead - she's gone with the wind and the dust and the worms - and Pierre Forveaux the father of lies Forveaux is still alive and kicking - the injustice of it!!!!!! - staggering - this is my darkest hour Sean - the cops are closing in - there's nowhere to run to nowhere to hide - it's all over bar the shouting - but you know what?

- I WON'T GO QUIETLY - no no a thousand times no - I'm not some faceless lump of cream cheese to be scooped up and slapped down on the poppy-seed bagel of their criminal justice system - not me not Trendy P: I'm working on my Exit Strategy

---

LINCOLN CENTER GUNMAN
LEAPS FROM BRIDGE

I know I know - jumping off a bridge = melodramatic / a cliché - don't worry Sean I've thought it through and I'm determined to make this a Stylish Exit: for starters I'll be wearing my Firebird Costume - the Firebird is basically an orange jumpsuit + pair of red wings on a balsa wood frame + a papier maché bird's head w/ a big golden (gold tinfoil really) beak - it was originally worn by the actor playing Lenny in a landmark avant-garde production of Pinter's *The Homecoming* that I directed off off B'way back in 1988 - I always wondered why I kept it - now I know - Tomorrow night Sean I shall return to Williamsburg Brooklyn (taking my last cab ride on earth) - I shall instruct the driver to drop me off at Driggs and S. 6th (or S. 7th ?) - I'll walk up the ramp and out on to the Williamsburg Bridge - yes the famous Williamsburg Bridge A.K.A. Sonny's woodshed - I will walk up the pedestrian walkway to the middle of the bridge and there don my wings and bird's head - next I douse wings and feathered breast with kerosene - then I climb out on to the outer struts of the bridge - here I am - can you see me hanging out over the black water? - at the stroke of midnight after reciting something apropos from *Les Fleurs du Mal* I strike a match and jump - very beautiful and very tragic: Trendy Prendy hanging for few brief seconds flapping my blazing wings in the night sky next to the neon Domino Sugar Factory sign - and then plunging down down down to kiss the water . . . This will be the last creative act of my life Sean: a sort of triple tribute to Igor Stravinsky and Baudelaire and Crawford the actor who jumped and upset all those tourists last Xmas - The only snag is getting the bird costume out of the storage hole - for his own sake that NYU snot had better not be on duty - if he stands in my way I'll peck his eyes out

———•———

Paid one last visit to my P.O. Box this morning - there was 1 piece of mail: a begging letter from an outfit called The Rescue Fund for Animals (Ireland) Ltd. asking for a donation to help 'all the neglected and abused cats and dogs of Ireland' - evidently news must have reached the Irish philanthropic underworld that I'm coming into money but the post being slow they don't know yet that I was gypped by aunties M and B - anyway it's your standard not-for-profit begging letter with whole paragraphs bolded in red dramatic underlining etc. - but there's one truly astonishing thing: The Signature - it gave me quite a jolt when I saw it Sean: the letter is signed 'For All The Cats and Dogs Of Ireland - Anne Marie Gerrity (Mrs.)' - Anne Marie Gerrity - Amelia Garrity - it's practically the same name isn't it? - I don't know Sean: to me it definitely feels like a wink from Beyond The Veil

———•———

February 1st: I'm thinking about The Last Will & Testament of Jarleth L. Prendergast - you're the only lawyer I've ever had dealings with who never did the dirt on me and as such I'd value your input with phrasing etc.

Item: To my friend and fellow animator Kenneth Privette: my editing table - it's broken but not beyond repair - all my unused stock - my samizdat copy of *Superstar: The Karen Carpenter Story* (which I stole from an obnoxious Soho couple who invited me to their snotty

snot loft party because they thought I was a friend of Harvey Keitel
- 6 Degrees of Stupidity!!!) - NB NB NB: Ken I want you to take all
my shorts + all my unfinished stuff and splice 'em all together - then
let the smelly dingo RUN!!!!

Untersturmführer Hans and The Animals (4 min.)
The Young Witch of Trim (6 min. Unfinished)
Oh God! The Vomit / Shroud of Turin (2 min. 8 sec.)
Those Who Hang Around Omelas and Get Shitfaced (3 min.)
Gumby's Big Score (10 min. Unfinished)
Make Me Come You White Bastard or I Kill You (4 min.)
Mr. Semtex Agent of Death in Toytown (28 min. Unfinished)
Die Frog Die! (notes and sketches)

Let Prendy's posthumous fart cloud explode in the faces of the Philistines!!

Item: To my wife Martha Suarez-Prendergast: Père Gumby A.K.A.
the Prince of Action Figures - Maybe I forgot to take him with me for
a reason - Anyway he's yours now - He likes it on top of the fridge: lord
of all he surveys etc. - Talk to him on long summer evenings Martha
- Tell him of your plans for a better mañana para todos los niños
- Let him take you in his strong green arms and sing you songs of
Gumbyland - of the brave knights and beauteous ladies of Gumbylot
in the olden times

Item: To Gwyneth Raptor: Gwyneth I behaved badly - most of the
stuff you bought me on your credit card is stashed at Acme Storage
on 2nd Ave. and 2nd St. - I'm sure if you explain the situation they'll
let you have it - no hard feelings and good luck with Mr. Muscles!

Item: To The Fund for Animals (Ireland) Ltd: - I hereby empower and command Aidan McGrath Solicitor to get up off his flabby West Brit arse and sell The Teapot (I actually DO remember it now funnily enough: I used to fill it up with Taylor Keith lemonade and drink out of the spout) - with monies gleaned from sale of said valuable (?) item I further empower and command him to write a cheque for X amount to The Rescue Fund for Animals (Ireland) Ltd. c/o Mrs. Anne Marie Gerrity President Millrace Farm Enniscorty Co. Wexford said Bequest to be known from this day forth as 'The Otto and Amelia Prendergast Perpetual Challenge Love Gift to The Cats and Dogs of Ireland' - it's a small gesture but hopefully it'll put me in Cerberus's good books - if it doesn't then fuck the begrudgers I'll come back as a porcupine - That's about it - Trendy P's affairs are all in order - Listen Sean I'm not much at saying goodbye - I look forward to shaking your hand on the Other Side - actually I hope to God there is no Other Side - having said that I want you to know I really appreciate your help and moral support all through STALKER and SNUFFOUT - you've stuck by me through a long and grim campaign - you're too modest to blow your own trumpet but I know there were times when things were going badly and you spoke up for me before the Throne of the Most High - i.e. you talked Father Odin out of blasting me with a thought-quick thunderbolt when I ripped Raptor off for the suit etc.- so it's hats off to you Sean Reynolds my home boy in the aether - cue Vera Lynn - there'll be bluebirds over - adieu my spirit guide adieu

———•———

2/2: It's nearly time to leave this strange savage place where the shop doors open out into the street and they carpet sections of the pavement and there are no public toilets and the fire engines and ambulances rocket by in broad daylight honking and clanking loud enough to wake the dead and every day sees an exponential growth in pompous morons barging down B'way barking into their cell phones - this strange savage place - where wives turn on their husbands at the slightest provocation and a shyster-fornicator can incite the love of your life to dance at the end of a rope - but it could be worse: you could wake up one morning and find you're a convict in Botany Bay in the 1800s and this morning it's your turn to get 200 lashes for filching a handful of dried rat turds from the warden's larder - no actually take it all in all New York's not such a bad place - I once saw Patrick McGoohan - The Prisoner - walking near the Dakota - another time in a pizzeria in midtown I saw the great Toshiro Mifune - or someone who looked incredibly like Mifune - Out of nowhere he jumped up on a table and started haranguing the customers - I still see those dark eyes flashing - THAT was a stirring sight - there's no doubt: I've seen some amazing things here and I've had some good laughs over the years

———·———

I feel happy - They say suicides go into a period of euphoria just before they actually do themselves in - I heard an interesting discussion about it one night on the box: they were talking about poor old Margaux Hemingway - all your friends are high fiving / patting themselves on the back because they've managed to keep you talking on the phone for an hr. or they tricked you into playing 10 games of chinese checkers and now you seem to be quite your old self again - 'I do believe she's turned the corner' etc. but next thing they know you're found swinging from a beam out in the stables - or in my case found floating in the East River - Apparently the euphoria comes when you stop dithering and decide to actually DO SOMETHING

———·———

To Officer O'Hara or the EMS guys or the boys at the morgue - whoever has the messy job of fishing me out toetagging me and putting me in a ziplock bag - I'd like to say sorry in advance for being a bother - jeez he sure is heavy - waterlogged the word is waterlogged - in closing I want to call on Mr. Charles Mingus & the Bellevue Observation Ward Choir to take us out with a spirited rendition of a fine old field shout 'Touch My Beloved's Thought While Her World's Affluence Crumbles At My Feet'

Remember Me This Way: standing in the rain in Herald's Square shaking my fist at the horrified punters on the top deck of a Big Apple Tours bus - captives waiting for the lights to change they stare down at me like frightened sheep as I give them an earful: KEEP MOVING - WE DON'T WANT YOU HERE - STUFF YOUR STINKING LIRA UP YOUR HOLE - GO BACK TO CHARTRES - GO BACK TO VERSAILLES - GO BACK TO BERLIN AND BRUSSELS AND BRUGE AND DON'T COME BACK - GO STRAIGHT TO HELL DO NOT PASS GO - WE ARE PUT ON EARTH A LITTLE SPACE THAT WE MAY LEARN TO BEAR THE BEAMS OF LOVE - HI HO SILVER AWAY

LANNAN SELECTIONS

The Lannan Foundation, located in Santa Fe, New Mexico, is a family foundation whose funding focuses on special cultural projects and ideas which promote and protect cultural freedom, diversity, and creativity.

The literary aspect of Lannan's cultural program supports the creation and presentation of exceptional English-language literature and develops a wider audience for poetry, fiction, and nonfiction.

Since 1990, the Lannan Foundation has supported Dalkey Archive Press projects in a variety of ways, including monetary support for authors, audience development programs, and direct funding for the publication of the Press's books.

In the year 2000, the Lannan Selections Series was established to promote both organizations' commitment to the highest expressions of literary creativity. The Foundation supports the publication of this series of books each year, and works closely with the Press to ensure that these books will reach as many readers as possible and achieve a permanent place in literature. Authors whose works have been published as Lannan Selections include Ishmael Reed, Stanley Elkin, Ann Quin, Nicholas Mosley, William Eastlake, and David Antin, among others.

PIERRE ALBERT-BIROT, *Grabinoulor.*
YUZ ALESHKOVSKY, *Kangaroo.*
FELIPE ALFAU, *Chromos.*
  Locos.
  Sentimental Songs.
IVAN ÂNGELO, *The Celebration.*
  The Tower of Glass.
ALAN ANSEN, *Contact Highs: Selected Poems 1957-1987.*
DAVID ANTIN, *Talking.*
DJUNA BARNES, *Ladies Almanack.*
  Ryder.
JOHN BARTH, *LETTERS.*
  Sabbatical.
ANDREI BITOV, *Pushkin House.*
LOUIS PAUL BOON, *Chapel Road.*
ROGER BOYLAN, *Killoyle.*
IGNÁCIO DE LOYOLA BRANDÃO, *Zero.*
CHRISTINE BROOKE-ROSE, *Amalgamemnon.*
BRIGID BROPHY, *In Transit.*
MEREDITH BROSNAN, *Mr. Dynamite.*
GERALD L. BRUNS,
  Modern Poetry and the Idea of Language.
GABRIELLE BURTON, *Heartbreak Hotel.*
MICHEL BUTOR, *Mobile.*
  Portrait of the Artist as a Young Ape.
JULIETA CAMPOS, *The Fear of Losing Eurydice.*
ANNE CARSON, *Eros the Bittersweet.*
CAMILO JOSÉ CELA, *The Family of Pascual Duarte.*
  The Hive.
LOUIS-FERDINAND CÉLINE, *Castle to Castle.*
  London Bridge.
  North.
  Rigadoon.
HUGO CHARTERIS, *The Tide Is Right.*
JEROME CHARYN, *The Tar Baby.*
MARC CHOLODENKO, *Mordechai Schamz.*
EMILY HOLMES COLEMAN, *The Shutter of Snow.*
ROBERT COOVER, *A Night at the Movies.*
STANLEY CRAWFORD, *Some Instructions to My Wife.*
ROBERT CREELEY, *Collected Prose.*
RENÉ CREVEL, *Putting My Foot in It.*
RALPH CUSACK, *Cadenza.*
SUSAN DAITCH, *L.C.*
  Storytown.
NIGEL DENNIS, *Cards of Identity.*
PETER DIMOCK,
  A Short Rhetoric for Leaving the Family.
ARIEL DORFMAN, *Konfidenz.*
COLEMAN DOWELL, *The Houses of Children.*
  Island People.
  Too Much Flesh and Jabez.
RIKKI DUCORNET, *The Complete Butcher's Tales.*
  The Fountains of Neptune.
  The Jade Cabinet.
  Phosphor in Dreamland.
  The Stain.
WILLIAM EASTLAKE, *The Bamboo Bed.*
  Castle Keep.
  Lyric of the Circle Heart.
JEAN ECHENOZ, *Chopin's Move.*
STANLEY ELKIN, *A Bad Man.*
  Boswell: A Modern Comedy.
  Criers and Kibitzers, Kibitzers and Criers.
  The Dick Gibson Show.
  The Franchiser.

  George Mills.
  The Living End.
  The MacGuffin.
  The Magic Kingdom.
  Mrs. Ted Bliss.
  The Rabbi of Lud.
  Van Gogh's Room at Arles.
ANNIE ERNAUX, *Cleaned Out.*
LAUREN FAIRBANKS, *Muzzle Thyself.*
  Sister Carrie.
LESLIE A. FIEDLER,
  Love and Death in the American Novel.
FORD MADOX FORD, *The March of Literature.*
CARLOS FUENTES, *Terra Nostra.*
  Where the Air Is Clear.
JANICE GALLOWAY, *Foreign Parts.*
  The Trick Is to Keep Breathing.
WILLIAM H. GASS, *The Tunnel.*
  Willie Masters' Lonesome Wife.
ETIENNE GILSON, *The Arts of the Beautiful.*
  Forms and Substances in the Arts.
C. S. GISCOMBE, *Giscome Road.*
  Here.
DOUGLAS GLOVER, *Bad News of the Heart.*
KAREN ELIZABETH GORDON, *The Red Shoes.*
PATRICK GRAINVILLE, *The Cave of Heaven.*
HENRY GREEN, *Blindness.*
  Concluding.
  Doting.
  Nothing.
JIŘÍ GRUŠA, *The Questionnaire.*
JOHN HAWKES, *Whistlejacket.*
AIDAN HIGGINS, *A Bestiary.*
  Flotsam and Jetsam.
  Langrishe, Go Down.
ALDOUS HUXLEY, *Antic Hay.*
  Crome Yellow.
  Point Counter Point.
  Those Barren Leaves.
  Time Must Have a Stop.
MIKHAIL IOSSEL AND JEFF PARKER, EDS.,
  *Amerika: Contemporary Russians View the
  United States.*
GERT JONKE, *Geometric Regional Novel.*
JACQUES JOUET, *Mountain R.*
DANILO KIŠ, *Garden, Ashes.*
  A Tomb for Boris Davidovich.
TADEUSZ KONWICKI, *A Minor Apocalypse.*
  The Polish Complex.
ELAINE KRAF, *The Princess of 72nd Street.*
JIM KRUSOE, *Iceland.*
EWA KURYLUK, *Century 21.*
VIOLETTE LEDUC, *La Bâtarde.*
DEBORAH LEVY, *Billy and Girl.*
  Pillow Talk in Europe and Other Places.
JOSÉ LEZAMA LIMA, *Paradiso.*
OSMAN LINS, *Avalovara.*
  The Queen of the Prisons of Greece.
ALF MAC LOCHLAINN, *The Corpus in the Library.*
  Out of Focus.
RON LOEWINSOHN, *Magnetic Field(s).*
D. KEITH MANO, *Take Five.*
BEN MARCUS, *The Age of Wire and String.*
WALLACE MARKFIELD, *Teitelbaum's Window.*
  To an Early Grave.

SELECTED DALKEY ARCHIVE PAPERBACKS

DAVID MARKSON, *Reader's Block.*
  Springer's Progress.
  Wittgenstein's Mistress.
CAROLE MASO, *AVA.*
LADISLAV MATEJKA AND KRYSTYNA POMORSKA, EDS.,
  Readings in Russian Poetics: Formalist and Structuralist
  Views.
HARRY MATHEWS,
  The Case of the Persevering Maltese: Collected Essays.
  Cigarettes.
  The Conversions.
  The Human Country: New and Collected Stories.
  The Journalist.
  Singular Pleasures.
  The Sinking of the Odradek Stadium.
  Tlooth.
  20 Lines a Day.
ROBERT L. McLAUGHLIN, ED.,
  Innovations: An Anthology of Modern &
    Contemporary Fiction.
STEVEN MILLHAUSER, *The Barnum Museum.*
  In the Penny Arcade.
RALPH J. MILLS, JR., *Essays on Poetry.*
OLIVE MOORE, *Spleen.*
NICHOLAS MOSLEY, *Accident.*
  Assassins.
  Catastrophe Practice.
  Children of Darkness and Light.
  The Hesperides Tree.
  Hopeful Monsters.
  Imago Bird.
  Impossible Object.
  Inventing God.
  Judith.
  Natalie Natalia.
  Serpent.
  The Uses of Slime Mould: Essays of Four Decades.
WARREN F. MOTTE, JR.,
  Fables of the Novel: French Fiction since 1990.
  Oulipo: A Primer of Potential Literature.
YVES NAVARRE, *Our Share of Time.*
WILFRIDO D. NOLLEDO, *But for the Lovers.*
FLANN O'BRIEN, *At Swim-Two-Birds.*
  At War.
  The Best of Myles.
  The Dalkey Archive.
  Further Cuttings.
  The Hard Life.
  The Poor Mouth.
  The Third Policeman.
CLAUDE OLLIER, *The Mise-en-Scène.*
FERNANDO DEL PASO, *Palinuro of Mexico.*
ROBERT PINGET, *The Inquisitory.*
RAYMOND QUENEAU, *The Last Days.*
  Odile.
  Pierrot Mon Ami.
  Saint Glinglin.
ANN QUIN, *Berg.*
  Passages.
  Three.
  Tripticks.
ISHMAEL REED, *The Free-Lance Pallbearers.*
  The Last Days of Louisiana Red.
  Reckless Eyeballing.
  The Terrible Threes.

  The Terrible Twos.
  Yellow Back Radio Broke-Down.
JULIÁN RÍOS, *Poundemonium.*
AUGUSTO ROA BASTOS, *I the Supreme.*
JACQUES ROUBAUD, *The Great Fire of London.*
  Hortense in Exile.
  Hortense Is Abducted.
  The Plurality of Worlds of Lewis.
  The Princess Hoppy.
  Some Thing Black.
LEON S. ROUDIEZ, *French Fiction Revisited.*
LUIS RAFAEL SÁNCHEZ, *Macho Camacho's Beat.*
SEVERO SARDUY, *Cobra & Maitreya.*
NATHALIE SARRAUTE, *Do You Hear Them?*
  Martereau.
ARNO SCHMIDT, *Collected Stories.*
  Nobodaddy's Children.
CHRISTINE SCHUTT, *Nightwork.*
GAIL SCOTT, *My Paris.*
JUNE AKERS SEESE,
  Is This What Other Women Feel Too?
  What Waiting Really Means.
AURELIE SHEEHAN, *Jack Kerouac Is Pregnant.*
VIKTOR SHKLOVSKY,
  A Sentimental Journey: Memoirs 1917-1922.
  Theory of Prose.
  Third Factory.
  Zoo, or Letters Not about Love.
JOSEF ŠKVORECKÝ,
  The Engineer of Human Souls.
CLAUDE SIMON, *The Invitation.*
GILBERT SORRENTINO, *Aberration of Starlight.*
  Blue Pastoral.
  Crystal Vision.
  Imaginative Qualities of Actual Things.
  Mulligan Stew.
  Pack of Lies.
  The Sky Changes.
  Something Said.
  Splendide-Hôtel.
  Steelwork.
  Under the Shadow.
W. M. SPACKMAN, *The Complete Fiction.*
GERTRUDE STEIN, *Lucy Church Amiably.*
  The Making of Americans.
  A Novel of Thank You.
PIOTR SZEWC, *Annihilation.*
ESTHER TUSQUETS, *Stranded.*
DUBRAVKA UGRESIC, *Thank You for Not Reading.*
LUISA VALENZUELA, *He Who Searches.*
BORIS VIAN, *Heartsnatcher.*
PAUL WEST, *Words for a Deaf Daughter & Gala.*
CURTIS WHITE, *Memories of My Father Watching TV.*
  Monstrous Possibility.
  Requiem.
DIANE WILLIAMS, *Excitability: Selected Stories.*
  Romancer Erector.
DOUGLAS WOOLF, *Wall to Wall.*
  Ya! & John-Juan.
PHILIP WYLIE, *Generation of Vipers.*
MARGUERITE YOUNG, *Angel in the Forest.*
  Miss MacIntosh, My Darling.
REYOUNG, *Unbabbling.*
LOUIS ZUKOFSKY, *Collected Fiction.*
SCOTT ZWIREN, *God Head.*

FOR A FULL LIST OF PUBLICATIONS, VISIT:
www.dalkeyarchive.com